A High Society Gangster thinks on a higher plane than most men. He operates off of a different set of principles. Loyalty and honor are at the root of his foundation. He knows no fear or boundaries in life. He exercises the power of his mind to control his brawn. He makes decisions based upon intellect and not emotions. He finds a way to make things happen against all odds. He does not know the meaning of the word defeat. He blazes the trail that others willingly follow.

------T. Long

High Society Gangster

Thomas Long

Prologue

With his gun in his hand, Geno wrapped his finger around the trigger and fired off several rounds in the direction of the individuals that were in hot pursuit of him and his brother, Silvio. His shots failed to hit any of the targets. Feeling hopeless, he sensed that the angel of death was about to call his name shortly. He wondered to himself how he let his older brother, Silvio, talk him into going along with this poorly thought out scheme. From the moment Silvio came to him with his plan, Geno's gut instinct told him it was a bad idea and he should have listened. However, he went along with it anyway because if they were able to pull the caper off, they stood to make a ton of grip to split between the two of them.

Geno's heart beat faster than the winning horse at the Kentucky Derby while bullets whistled by him when he peaked his head up from behind the dumpster. He hoped and prayed that his life wasn't about to come to an end at just seventeen years old. Fear was a natural feeling to have in a time like this, but he couldn't let it show. He had to man up and go out on his shield like a soldier. As things stood, they were trapped at the end of an alley with only one way out and that path was blocked off by several young, angry Black men toting some serious firearms. They were outnumbered and outgunned. The situation looked bleak for them, but to throw in the white flag to surrender was not an option.

"It ain't no need to be scared now, G. This is the type of action that I live for all day, every day. This is that shit that will put some hair on your chest, little brother. You're finally getting a chance to earn your stripes by putting in some real work. Don't worry about a thing because I'ma get us out of here," Silvio spit out confidently. He had taught Geno how to properly shoot a gun, but this was his first time actually being involved in a real live gun battle. Thus far, Geno held his own like he expected him to do. After all, he was a Caprese and anything less than being a thoroughbred was unacceptable.

"I'm not scared, Sil. I'm just mad that I followed you into this alley instead of running the other way because I wouldn't be in this situation right now. If I get out of this situation alive, I'ma kick your ass," Geno promised him. Bullets continued to fly in their direction, but none of them found their mark. Geno peeped cautiously around the side of the dumpster and let off a few more rounds from his gun.

Silvio and Geno argued like this all of the time. Brotherly competition was an inherent part of their relationship with one another. They both always wanted to one up the other in everything they did. At this time in their young lives, Silvio and Geno considered themselves to be young gangsters in training. They were on a mission to earn respect out in the streets at any cost. Silvio was the more ambitious and brave hearted of the two brothers whereas Geno was more of the laid back, calculated thinker even at his young age. Even though they often bumped heads, they were still family. Silvio could talk slick and criticize Geno all he wanted to, but nobody else in their neighborhood better try to because he would be quick to lay hands on them. The same held true for Geno. The Caprese boys had already earned a reputation for being two hard-nosed bad boys in their Little Italy community.

Outside of stealing cars or breaking into homes, selling weed was their major hustle. They had a small customer base that consisted of local high school kids that they grew up with and a few drifters from their little Italy neighborhood. They made close to two grand a week to split between them and their two partners in crime, Sal and Cappi. They copped their marijuana from a young Black drug dealer in northwest Baltimore who went by the name Butterball. His real name was Jerome, but his friends called him by this nickname because of his portly shaped body. He was a shade over five feet and six inches tall, with a belly that hung over his pants. He was the top dope dealer in his area and not only sold marijuana, but also heroin and cocaine. After watching his operation for a few weeks, Silvio saw how much money his crew made and came up with the brilliant idea to try and rob him. He observed that Butterball stashed the drugs and money at the house where he lived.

Silvio decided that tonight was the night to make his move on him because he saw this as the perfect opportunity to make his first major power move in the streets to take his street credibility to the next level. Sal and Cappi knew that Butterball's crew was heavily armed and saw the plan as a suicide mission. They wanted no parts of something so insane. Silvio, ever the risk taker, was undeterred to pull of this big score. He talked Geno into joining him by using the honor of the Caprese name as his trump card. Their father was a fearless gangster in his heyday and he told Geno that he would be proud of them for having the balls to pull off this caper. That was all the convincing he needed to do to get him to go all in with him because to gain his father's approval was his first mission in life.

When they made their move on Butterball's stash house, Silvio kicked in the front door with his gun drawn. Butterball was seated on the sofa with his pants around his ankles having oral sex performed on him by a random crackhead female from the neighborhood. With Geno and Silvio's guns pointed in his direction, his fear of death made Butterball give up the location of his money and product quickly. He kept his money underneath his bed in a shoebox.

When Geno retrieved the shoebox, it contained close to twenty-five grand, wrapped up in several rubber bands. Butterball stored his drug stash in the ceiling panel above his bed. The amount of drugs that he had in his stash had a street value of close to twenty grand. To get away with forty-five stacks was a damn good lick for two thirsty Italian kids from the other side of town. When they were about to make their escape, they had no clue that one of Butterball's boys saw them kick in his door and quickly rounded up their troops for backup. When they stepped out of the front door of Butterball's house, Silvio and Geno were greeted by a pack of angry, young Black men armed with some serious firepower and ready to get it on.

Unphased by the fact that they were in Butterball's home turf and outnumbered by his boys, Silvio displayed the heart of a soldier when he let off rounds from his gun in their direction. They scattered like roaches for cover and hid behind cars on the street. Their brief retreat gave him and Geno just enough time to bolt through Butterball's yard into the alley. As they ran, the angry mob was right behind them in hot pursuit, with guns drawn and shots firing from every direction. They both ran down the alley in a zigzag pattern in an attempt to avoid getting hit. It took a moment before they realized that the alley had only one way out and that was back in the direction from which they just came. If they wanted to survive, they only had one option- hide behind the dumpster and try to shoot their way out.

"You might as well lay down them guns now White boys. Y'all ain't leaving out of here alive tonight. You picked the wrong niggas to fuck with," one of Butterball's crew yelled from the top of the alley. The gunfire ceased for a moment before a hail of bullets was sent in Silvio and Geno's direction.

"Fuck you, niggas. We ain't giving up shit," Silvio replied defiantly. He stood up from behind the dumpster and fired shots from the two Glocks he held in his hands. This wasn't his first time firing a gun. He went to the gun range on a regular and was a damn good shot. His bullets hit a few of his opponents because he saw one of them laid out on the ground and heard another one of them scream out loud in pain.

Geno wasn't religious, but he prayed like never before that God would get him out of this mess alive. He swore that he would never let Silvio talk him into another hair brain scheme like this one again. Being involved in this kind of caper went against Geno's high level of intellect and normally rational thinking mind. Silvio was all brawn and approached things like he could always get his self out of any situation by exerting brute force. However, what he wasn't prepared for was an opponent who could match or exceed his force such as in the situation which they found themselves in currently.

"Okay, if that's how you want it, but you're going to die tonight," the same young soldier yelled. His words were followed up by more gunfire.

After another round of heated exchange, Butterball's crew noticed that Geno and Silvio no longer returned fire in their direction. They figured that they were out of ammunition and trapped behind the dumpster. At that moment, the leader of Butterball's crew motioned for the five remaining soldiers to follow behind him so they could move in on Geno and Silvio and kill them execution style. That was the wrong move. Silvio and Geno were playing possum.

When Butterball's crew made their way down the alley in plain view, with their guns drawn, Silvio hopped up from behind the dumpster and proceeded to fire his weapon. Geno followed suit. When it was all said and done, Butterball's soldiers lay dead in the alley from the onslaught of bullets that came in their direction. Silvio and Geno retrieved the drugs and money they stole and headed down the alley to make their escape. They could hear the police sirens getting closer. They ran in the direction of the unmarked car they left parked on a side street and hopped inside.

"That's what I'm talking about, G. We did that shit, man! We pulled it off!" Silvio said excitedly. He was amped up that they were able to get away without a scratch on them and with a gang of money in tow. He already had a buyer set up to purchase the drugs they stole and his split of the cash made him feel like he couldn't be touched right now. He drove the speed limit down the street so as not to draw attention to them. He noticed the police cars with their sirens on ride right past them in the direction of the gunshots. He let out a huge sigh of relief that they were in the clear. Geno silently thanked God for saving his life.

"Man that was some dumb shit we just did. We could've gotten killed," Geno argued.

"Yeah, but we didn't so stop your whining. If you're feeling some kind of way about this, I will gladly keep your take from the job," Silvio responded.

"The hell if you will, Sil. I earned my take fair and square. You're missing my point. You just don't get it, do you? As always, you miss the big picture," Geno stated. It was pointless for him to elaborate because Silvio wouldn't understand. Instead, he closed his eyes and sat quietly to collect his thoughts. This would be the last time he put himself in such a dangerous position. He didn't plan to give up the gangster lifestyle because that was what he was born to be. It was in his blood. However, from this point on, he would do things differently. He would be smarter with how he conducted business in the streets, unlike his gung ho brother.

Chapter 1

From the moment he woke up, Geno knew this would be another good day for him. For the first time in a while, he was able to get a full eight hours of sleep. The rest he just got made him feel like a new man. He felt refreshed and re-energized. The last few weeks were rough on him because he had several high profile cases to litigate back to back. As a result, he spent endless hours strategizing with his legal team to prepare the best defense possible for his clients. The late nights at the office left him with bags under his eyes and feeling mentally drained. Truth be told, he needed a nice Caribbean vacation to relax for a few weeks. He planned to do just that, with his family, once things settled down. Until then, he would have to tough it out.

When Geno turned over to his right side, he noticed that his bed was empty. His wife,

Carina, saw that he was sleeping so peacefully and didn't want to wake him up when she got up. Instead, she went about her business quietly and went downstairs to make breakfast for Geno and their children before they went to work and school respectively. Geno looked over at the clock on his nightstand and was stunned to see it was almost seven-thirty. He was usually out of the house by seven o'clock so he could be at the office at no later than eight o'clock sharp. However, he felt relieved when he remembered he wasn't headed into the office today because he had to be in court this morning by ten o'clock.

Geno got up out of the bed and let out a loud yawn while he stretched his limbs. He walked into the bathroom to relieve himself. When he was done, he let his boxers drop to the floor and took off his wife beater t-shirt so that he could take a shower. After he showered and shaved, he strolled over to his walk-in closet to pick out a fresh suit to wear for the day. Once his selection was made, he took his time getting dressed.

Geno paid close attention to every detail of his attire so that every piece of clothing hung from his body perfectly. To him, physical appearance was of the utmost importance. Whenever he went out into the public, Geno was the kind of man that women would do a double take to check out. He was always sharply dressed and had a confidence in his stride that was hard to ignore. He walked over to his jewelry valet to retrieve his platinum wedding band. He carefully slid it on his finger. Next, he had to make sure that he put on the right watch to compliment his ensemble. He selected his Rolex Oyster Perpetual line watch to wear today. The shiny diamond hour markers on it were elegant, but not too flashy. This type of watch should only be worn by a man with the right amount of swagger and style to compliment such a fine timepiece. The watch made a statement that its owner had good taste in watches. It was a gift from Carina for his thirtieth birthday. He felt it brought him good luck, which was just what he needed today.

He splashed on a dash of Gucci cologne and aftershave lotion. He loved to smell good at all times even if he lounged around the house. To complete his ensemble, he slid on a pair of Giuseppe loafers. He looked as dapper as could be. He exited his bedroom and walked down the long hallway toward the spiraling staircase. Once he was on the first level of his mansion, he headed toward the kitchen to grab a cup of coffee for a much needed burst of energy. He could hear the clanging sound of pots and pans from afar. When he reached the kitchen, he saw his beautiful wife, Carina. She busied herself making breakfast for their children, Gianna and Stefan. His children were preoccupied with their Ipads at the kitchen table while she cooked.

"Good morning, family," he stated in an animated tone. He walked over and gently kissed Carina on the cheek. Gianna and Stefan both spoke and got back to what they were doing on their Ipads. Like most of the youth today, they were too engrossed in their cyber world to have time for their parents. He walked over to the coffee machine to turn it on.

"I'm glad you finally woke up and decided to join us for breakfast," Carina replied jokingly. She smiled from ear to ear when she saw Geno. It gave her goose bumps to see him dressed in a suit. She felt blessed to have such a handsome man to call her own. With each passing day, her love for him grew stronger.

"I can't do breakfast today, honey. I have to be in court by ten and I'm running late. This is a big day for me. I have a lot riding on this case. I'll just take this cup of coffee and be on my way. However, before I go, how about you bring your little sweet rear end over here and give your old man a kiss for good luck," Geno requested.

Carina visibly looked disappointed. She genuinely cherished every moment that her entire family spent together and hoped that he could join them for breakfast. Over the years, it bothered her, at times, that he had to spend so many hours away from home. A part of her wished he had a regular nine to five job so she could count on him being home more often for dinner. However, she knew Geno had important business to tend to so she didn't complain. Besides, she knew what she signed up for when she married him. Geno Caprese let her know from the beginning he had dreams and aspirations that superseded those of the average man and would do whatever was necessary to bring them into fruition.

"Anything for you, babes. Knock'em dead today, honey," Carina replied. She did as Geno requested and gave him a kiss on the lips. Geno wrap his arms around her waist. Stefan and Gianna looked disgusted to see their parents show each other affection. Like most children, they felt that they were too old to be engaged in such acts.

"You know I will. I always do. Once I turn on that Caprese charm, I'll have the jury eating out of the palm of my hands. You kids have a good day in school," Geno stated enthusiastically like a proud parent. He walked over to Stefan and ruffled up his hair. He leaned over and kissed Gianna on her cheek. She pulled away and wiped her cheek with her hand. Geno just laughed at them. Truthfully, his children loved him to death and worshipped the ground that he walked on. Geno grabbed his keys off of the counter, picked up his leather briefcase that was situated by the front door, and headed outside to hop in his car.

Chapter 2

When Geno walked outside, he was greeted by the brightness of the sun. This was the first day of spring and it was almost eighty degrees outside. He threw on his Gucci sunglasses to block out the sun rays and hopped inside of his car. He drove down the winding driveway toward the front gate where his security team was stationed. He paid a hefty amount of money to have the best video surveillance equipment installed all around his property. A man of his wealthy stature required around the clock security for his family to keep them safe from harm. As he approached the gate, one of his armed guards, Vinny, stepped out of the booth to greet him. Geno rolled down his window to speak.

"Hey, Vinny, how's it going today?" he asked.

"It's all good, Mr. C," he replied.

"That's what I like to hear."

Vinny hit the button to allow for the gate to open so that Geno could make his exit out on to the street. Geno mashed his foot on the gas and sped off. He enjoyed the pleasant breeze while he drove down the highway. He now had his windows fully rolled down and the top open on his bright red Corvette. For the entire ride, his mind revisited all of his legal maneuvers, step by step, in his current case to make sure he didn't miss an important detail that could help him gain an acquittal for his clients. While he pondered the specific details of the case, he searched for something to listen to on the radio. It was just him and the open road. He had totally blocked out all of the cars that surrounded him on both sides. He was in his own zone.

After he drove for close to thirty minutes, he got off at his exit in downtown Baltimore. He weaved through traffic in the direction of the parking garage near the courthouse where he normally parked his car. He pulled into the underground lot and got out to hand his keys to the parking attendant. He had a five minute journey to make it to the courthouse. Geno felt confident that he had covered every detail that needed to be addressed in the case and he had no cause for worry or concern. Once he was inside of the courthouse, he greeted the security guards with a pleasant smile and proceeded to go through the metal detector. When he cleared security, he briskly strolled toward the courtroom where his case was being heard. He took a deep breath before he entered the courtroom. Once inside, he made his way to the front and took his seat next to his clients.

Geno sat back in his chair and looked as cool, calm, and composed as ever. His navy blue tailor made suit hung just right from his five foot, eight inch slender frame. On the surface, his head full of curly hair and pretty boy good looks made him appear harmless and innocent. Truth be told, he was a pit bull in disguise because once he sprung into action, his true colors showed quickly. As a defense attorney, he was as vicious as they came. He vigilantly defended all of his clients to ensure they received a fair and impartial trial. Geno's ability to break down witnesses on the stand and to call into question their credibility was unmatched.

A natural born orator, he was normally able to convincingly argue on behalf of his clients to, at the very least, raise a reasonable doubt or get a full acquittal on all charges. Opposing prosecutors hated to see him walk into the courtroom with the defendant they sought to convict because they knew they were in for an all out battle. Not only was Geno an effective litigator, but he also had a team of paralegals, private investigators, and subject matter experts on his payroll that armed him with the necessary tools to wage war on behalf of his clients. If push came to shove, he wasn't above paying off the Judge or a jury member if the situation called for such extreme actions for him to leave out with a victory. He did whatever it took to prevail in court. He was every prosecutor's worst nightmare, but every defendant's guardian angel.

Geno's cocky demeanor could easily be mistaken for arrogance. However, to call Geno arrogant would suggest that the high level of confidence he had in his ability as an attorney to be able to guarantee his clients would routinely walk out of the courtroom with their freedom was unmerited. Nothing was further from the truth. Geno Caprese happened to be the top defense attorney in the state of Maryland by far. He earned that reputation honestly by winning some of the toughest legal battles, with both state and federal prosecutors, for his clients for more than a decade. He took on multiple high profile drug and murder cases that involved notorious individuals who had a history of antisocial behavior. By the time he was done arguing on their behalf, he made them appear to the jury as victims of a corrupt police department that had conspired to set them up to take a fall. He truly understood how influential the power of perception was to sway the opinion of a jury and worked every angle he could to get his desired outcome.

Not only was he a force to be reckoned with in criminal cases, Geno was even more effective as an attorney in civil cases. He successfully litigated several police brutality and harassment cases that were filed against various police officers across the state of Maryland and won six and seven figure settlements for his clients. He was able to secure lofty settlements as well for many of his clients who filed wrongful termination suits against their former employers.

Most of his civil cases never made it to court and were settled amicably beforehand because his legal opponents didn't relish the thought of going up against him in court. Geno was intellectually intimidating to most of his colleagues in the legal profession even though they possessed equally as impressive credentials. Geno had that X factor that made him stand out from the crowd. His mental edge over them couldn't be described adequately in words, but it was clearly evident. He cast a dark cloud over his foes whenever he walked into a courtroom.

Geno graduated from Georgetown University Law School at the top of his class. He was highly sought after by numerous big law firms once he passed the bar, but he turned them and the high six figure salaries they offered him down, without a second thought. He opted instead to start his own private practice so he could be his own boss. He didn't need their money or reputations in the legal community to help him establish himself. Geno was a natural born leader who knew how to influence and persuade people to do what he wanted them to do.

Now that he had the academic credentials and a thorough knowledge of the legal system in his repertoire, he saw success as the inevitable result of his efforts. He knew he had what it took to be successful as an attorney from the time he decided in the tenth grade that was what he wanted to pursue in life. He used to love to read news articles about the legendary attorney Bruce Cutler, who was successful for many years in getting acquittals for the late John Gotti on a host of charges. He went to the library to pull up court transcripts of his most prominent cases. He loved the charismatic way he went about persuading a jury to see things his way. Cutler was a general in the courtroom and Geno modeled his courtroom mannerisms after his style.

Geno Caprese also had other factors that worked to his advantage. He wasn't your average struggling law student who needed assistance to make a name for himself. He was already well known throughout Baltimore City, but not for his academic achievements. Allegedly, he was a second generation Italian gangster with heavy ties to the criminal underworld of Baltimore City. It was reported that he sat at the head of one of the city's most highly organized crime families along with his older brother, Silvio. However, that allegation was never proven in a court of law and for anyone to claim it as being factual would be considered as slanderous. Geno was always locked and loaded, ready to sue for monetary damages for defamation of his character or his family's name. Geno projected an image of himself to the public that he was just another hard working, law abiding Italian American citizen who found a way to take advantage of every opportunity available in a free enterprise society to be able to afford to live a good life filled with all of the best amenities and luxury items this world had to offer.

In spite of all the allegations that were made about his criminal ties, Geno was still universally respected by his legal peers. They all had to appreciate his legal skills and admire his brilliance. He made the impossible become possible and made a light appear in the darkest of legal circumstances. If he took his client's money to defend them, he could bet the house that he would either walk out of the courtroom with a not guilty verdict or a plea bargain for a far lesser sentence than what the prosecution sought. Geno was just that damn good at his job and had no problem letting it be known. That was why his legal fees were so high.

His face was plastered on billboards all over the city that advertised his legal services. He also ran radio and television commercials to further publicize his law firm. Attorneys that were far older and more seasoned in the field were forced to acknowledge this young superstar in the making. They had to give him his props, whether they wanted to or not.

"How is it going today, my friend? You look a little uptight. You should relax a little," Geno uttered when he glanced over at the federal prosecutor, Gavin Mayhem, and cracked a slight grin. He covered his mouth with his hand while he yawned to suggest that he was bored and not impressed by all of Mayhem's legal maneuvers that he used throughout their current trial in his attempt to convict his clients and good friends, Jarvis and Milton Jackson.

"You are such a prick," Prosecutor Mayhem stated with sheer venom in his voice. He was hardly amused by Geno's antics. He hated him with a passion for both personal and professional reasons. He sat stone faced and attempted to win a stare down with Geno, but it didn't work. Geno knew he had this case in the bag and that he could add another victory notch to his belt to further enhance his impressive resume. All he needed was for the jury to handle its part of the deal and make it official.

"Well, there was a time your daughter had a different opinion of me. Please send her my regards," Geno shot back at him sarcastically.

Mayhem's face turned beat red. He was heated. He clinched his fists tightly. He shot Geno an evil stare. He wanted to strangle him with his bare hands to wipe that smug grin off of his face. He saw Geno as nothing more than a grimy criminal dressed up in a fancy suit. For him to be allowed to practice law made a mockery of the American criminal justice system.

Over the years, no matter how hard he tried, he could never prove a case against Geno or any of his alleged associates, but he was determined to do so before he retired. His pure hatred for his supposed involvement in organized crime wasn't the only reason he couldn't stand Geno. His dislike for him was of a more deeply rooted personal nature.

Geno used to date Mayhem's daughter, Amy. They met while they were both students in the pre-law program at Loyola University. She was now a successful attorney in her own right with her own practice that specialized in auto personal injury, labor and employment disputes, and bankruptcy cases. Geno broke her heart when he dumped her out of the blue to marry his wife, Carina. She had no clue that Geno happened to be dating both of them at the same time.

Amy suffered a nervous breakdown and went through a long period of depression after Geno decided to tell her about Carina when he found out she was pregnant. When she learned the man she loved and committed herself to was about to marry another woman, Amy was devastated to say the least. It took her years of psychotherapy to recover from her heartbreak and disappointment. Mayhem swore to pay Geno back for the emotional pain and trauma he caused his baby girl. He was there for every step of her recovery process to help her get back on her feet. Every time he saw Geno, he was filled with venom and thoughts of revenge for what he did to Amy. If he could get away with it, he wouldn't mind putting a bullet right between Geno's eyes to send him straight to hell, where he felt he deserved to go for all of his evil deeds.

"I oughta kick your butt, you little Italian punk," Mayhem threatened.

"I would advise you to reconsider, my friend. Don't let your little feelings get you in over your head. Please watch it with the ethnic slurs. That is so petty of you," Geno replied calmly, but in a firm tone. He was getting a cheap thrill out of ruffling Mayhem's feathers.

Even though Mayhem's six foot, well built frame towered over him, Geno showed no fear that he would do him physical harm. Geno used to be an amateur boxer and was lethal with his hands. He had carved up guys bigger than Mayhem with ease in his younger days. A fifty something year old man stood no chance against an athletic young stud like Geno. In spite of his outward display of bravado, Mayhem himself knew this to be true. Nonetheless, Mayhem stood up like he was about to lunge at Geno, but the assistant prosecutor, Niles Jennings, tapped him on his shoulder to bring him back to reality. He had to remind him they were in a court of law and he had to remain as professional as possible, no matter what Geno did to push his buttons. Mayhem gradually calmed down and sat back down in his seat. He had to refocus himself on the task at hand.

Shortly, he hoped that the judge would return to the bench and call the courtroom to order. At that time, they both would find out what the verdict would be in the Jackson brothers' case. Even though Mayhem saw pieces of his case unravel, he still held on to hope that he could still win a conviction. It would be the sweetest revenge for him to be able to win the case and to rub it in Geno's face. He glanced over at Geno engaged in conversation with his clients. The relaxed manner in which they conversed suggested that they didn't have a care in the world. Mayhem prayed they were wrong.

Chapter 3

Jarvis Jackson looked straight ahead at the judge the whole time he was in the courtroom today and throughout the entire trial. His stare gave off an icy cold, emotionless vibe like he was not at all fazed by the entire legal proceeding. He showed no fear whatsoever that he faced life in prison. That was because he was a soldier and whatever went down, he was prepared to face the music like a man. He also had supreme confidence in Geno that he would deliver an acquittal as promised. Conversely, Milton Jackson took the situation a slight bit more seriously. He didn't doubt Geno's ability to beat the charges against them, but he also knew to beat a federal drug case was a crapshoot that could go either way. He prayed heavily that the pendulum of justice swung in their favor.

"Geno, why is the jury taking so long to come back with the verdict?" Milton asked him anxiously.

"Relax your nerves, Milton; it's just a part of the process. The fact that they took so long to debate the facts of this case is a good thing for you guys. It means that they see some issues with the prosecutor's case. I've seen this enough times to not feel concerned at all. I've got this under control," Geno reassured him.

""Yeah, Milton, Geno is on his job. We're going home today. There is no need for us to worry about a thing, bro," Jarvis predicted boldly. Geno nodded in his direction to acknowledge and appreciate his vote of confidence.

The case that Geno was in court for now was another high profile one that garnered heavy media attention. It didn't faze Geno because he loved the spotlight. He always had a witty sound bite to give the press when they bombarded him with questions about his clients. It made Geno feel proud when he came home from a long day in court and his children would greet him at the door excited to tell him that they saw him on the news. Geno knew how to work the media to use them as an asset to help his clients gain an acquittal. He understood the power of the media to influence public opinion and meticulously chose his words when he addressed them. He had already defied the odds by getting both brothers released on bail despite the prosecutor's attempt to have them bound over until the trial began due to the serious nature of the charges that were leveled against them. Both of their bails were set at a half million dollars, but they had the financial resources to pay that easily.

Milton and Jarvis Jackson were arrested, along with a slew of others allegedly involved in their drug ring, and charged with conspiracy to distribute heroin and cocaine, arranging multiple drug related murders, and with running a continuing criminal enterprise. The federal government alleged that the brothers ran a drug organization over the last decade in East Baltimore that employed over one hundred individuals and generated almost eleven million dollars in illegal profits annually. They contended that Jarvis and Milton arranged to have several individuals within their drug organization killed when it was discovered they had become informants.

They were also being charged with using drug money to fund several businesses they owned in the names of other individuals. If convicted of the charges, they both faced life in prison. The fact that the federal government had an overall ninety-three percent conviction rate in all federal cases didn't matter to Geno. The Jackson brothers paid him almost a million dollars in legal fees to defend them. He planned to make sure they walked on all charges no matter what it took. He pulled out all of the stops and used every weapon at his disposal to make it happen. Losing was not an option for that amount of money.

When the DEA arrested the brothers, it was all over the news. Images of a gang of young Black men being handcuffed and placed in the back of paddy wagons were on full display during the daily newscasts for all to view. Several kilograms of heroin and cocaine, over a half a million dollars in cash, and a slew of handguns and assault rifles were seized in the raids that were conducted on various stash houses throughout the city. All of the seized evidence was put on display at the press conference for all to see. The press conference was an attempt on the part of the current mayor of Baltimore City, James Roberts, and the Police Commissioner, Herman Leftwich, to send a message to the public that law enforcement was serious about its efforts to reduce drug related crime in the City. They planned to make an example out of the Jackson brothers, but Geno had a strategy of his own to counter their attempt.

The Jackson brothers had been on the DEA's radar for several years, but they had yet to gather enough evidence to charge them with a crime. Even with this arrest, they had no hard evidence of either of them handling drugs directly or any recorded conversations where they discussed any drug transactions. Milton and Jarvis were too smart to be caught doing something so foolish. The only thing that the government had on them was the testimony of several of the other individuals they previously arrested on minor drug charges who claimed to be affiliated with the Jackson brothers as a part of their organization.

These individuals agreed to become cooperating witnesses or snitches as they were more appropriately called in the streets. Some of them were on probation or parole already and this was used as leverage to get them to cooperate because none of them wanted to go back to jail. The informants gave up the locations of several of the Jackson crew's stash houses, but couldn't get either brother to talk about drug activity directly over a wiretap.

Geno had a field day destroying the credibility of the government's witnesses in front of the jury. He was convinced that he had swayed the jury to believe that the informants implicated his clients in the drug ring in exchange for them receiving a lighter sentence for the crimes for which they were being charged. He did his best to send home the message that the prosecutor used it as leverage to get them to implicate two innocent men in crimes that the government had no hard evidence to connect them with at all.

Mayhem's case took a heavy blow when his star witness, Pharrell Edmonds, alias Big P, disappeared before he could be secured away in witness protection until he testified in court. Big P was one of the Jackson brothers top lieutenants in the organization and his testimony would have been hard to overcome because he knew everything about the inner workings of their drug empire. The federal agents had a tail on him for several months during their investigation and were able to arrest him with two kilograms of crack cocaine in his possession after he left one of the organization's stash houses en route to replenish the drug supply of their street level dealers. Big P had already served seven years in federal jail for a prior drug distribution charge and another conviction would have landed him an even lengthier bid. His last incarceration took a toll on him mentally and emotionally. His father and one of his daughters died while he was locked up and he was unable to see them before they passed away. He was determined to not go back behind the wall again.

When Mayhem offered him immunity and to put him in the U.S. Federal Witness Protection program in exchange for testifying against his lifelong friends and business partners, the Jackson brothers, he jumped at the deal. It was an offer that he couldn't refuse. That was why they were surprised he bailed out before he got a chance to take advantage of his get out of jail free card. His disappearing act didn't add up, but there was nothing that Mayhem could do. He issued an arrest warrant for Big P, but he was in the wind and nowhere to be found. To try and still win the case, he had to rely on the testimony of the other members of the organization that he successfully flipped.

However, they were all street level dealers and none of them had direct access to the Jackson brothers' illegal dealings like Big P did. With his star witness missing in action, Mayhem had to work with what little bit of evidence he had. He knew he faced an uphill battle, but remained optimistic.

Chapter 4

Jarvis and Milton Jackson were identical twins in their early thirties. Jarvis was the older of the two by seven minutes. The only way to tell them apart was that Jarvis wore his hair in dreads and Milton always kept a bald head. They weren't your average drug dealers who fit into the prototyped image of the inner city raised young Black male who came from a broken home and had limited education and options to achieve success in life. Raised in the Parkville area, they came from a suburban family with both parents in the home. They never wanted for anything growing up because their parents, Emile and Carol Ann Jackson, were in a financial position to be able to provide them with anything they desired. However, as they got older, they learned quickly that not even their community was immune from the impact of drugs and crime.

As teenagers, they saw that the kids in their suburban neighborhood loved to smoke marijuana, sniff cocaine, and drink alcohol just as much as their inner city counterparts. The difference was that the suburban kids had trust funds and weekly allowances to buy drugs and alcohol while the inner city kids had to resort to crime most of the time to support their drug habits.

The Jackson brothers grew up watching movies like *Menace to Society, Boyz in the Hood, Juice,* and *New Jack City* and became fascinated with the drug culture. They fell in love with the flashy clothes and jewelry, as well as the powerful persona of characters like Nino Brown and Old Dog, and sought to emulate them. Jarvis was the bolder of the two brothers and one day decided to take a trip into the inner city to try and find a drug connection where he could buy drugs wholesale to resell in their neighborhood to their friends in school. He lucked up and managed to be introduced to a drug dealer by the name of Harvey who sold him his first ounce of weed. Jarvis and Milton got rid of that first ounce of weed by lunch time at school the next day.

They couldn't believe how fast they had turned a profit on their minimal investment. In less than a few months, they were able to buy pounds of weed to sell to not only their friends in school, but also to some of their parents who loved to get high as well. After they made a good amount of money from selling weed, they ventured off into selling cocaine and heroin to increase their profits. They started off buying ounces of product and moved on to being able to purchase kilos of medium grade product. Pretty soon, they had the entire area on lockdown. As business continued to pick up, they expanded their territory and had a solid crew working for them all across East Baltimore. Despite their success in the drug trade, they knew that it wouldn't last forever. They had a well thought out exit strategy. Selling drugs was just an illegal means to achieve a legitimate end.

Their parents had no clue about their illegal activities the entire time. That was because while their drug business was in full swing, they both maintained good grades in school and were discreet with how they conducted their business. After they finished high school, they both enrolled in college classes at Loyola University. Milton graduated with a Bachelor's degree in Accounting and Jarvis obtained his degree in Business Management. It was at college where they first became affiliated by chance with Geno.

They all met at a fraternity party and instantly struck up a friendship. Over time, they noticed that they had similar criminal interests. They sold drugs and Geno had the connection to drug suppliers that could get them work at far cheaper prices than what they paid Harvey for his product. Consequently, they put their heads together and worked out a mutually beneficial business relationship where they could all make a gang of money legally and illegally.

As college educated thugs, they all planned to have the best of both worlds. They all knew that their illegal activities wouldn't last forever because it would only be a matter of time before they made a mistake somewhere along the line and got caught by the law. Consequently, they mapped out an exit strategy that included a hostile takeover of corporate America. Thus far, all of the pieces of their plan fell into place perfectly.

After they graduated from college, the Jackson brothers managed to obtain a small business loan so that they could open up a clothing apparel store called Urban Gear Central. The store sold the latest in name brand urban gear and apparel from all of the hottest fashion designers. It was located in White Marsh Mall and the store was the perfect cover for their illegal drug activities because it generated a significant amount of legitimate income for them which they used to open up several other businesses throughout the city. When Geno obtained his law degree and passed the bar, his legal expertise came in handy to keep their criminal enterprise out of the reach of the legal system.

To create a positive public image, the brothers donated generously to various non-profit organizations and churches throughout the city. They gave away food baskets for Thanksgiving and purchased thousands of dollars worth of toys every Christmas season for families in need. They joined the Board of Directors of several non-profit organizations to bolster their image of being committed to serving the community. They were also active members of the biggest AME church in the black community. They both attended church services religiously every Sunday. It was their way of atoning for their sins.

Their acts of kindness and generosity made them revered and respected in the Black community. To the public, they looked like choirboys as opposed to the vicious drug lords they actually were. They gave substantial financial contributions to the political campaigns of several prestigious local politicians that helped them gain their political seats. Several community leaders and high profile ministers testified on their behalf as character witnesses during the trial.

After all of the legal wrangling and maneuvering over the past few months, today would be the day that their fate would be decided. The jury had debated for the past three days and had finally reached a verdict. Milton and Jarvis were ready to face the music however things turned out. Geno was as calm as Floyd Mayweather was when it was fight night and he stared down his opponent in the center of the ring. Just like Floyd was the undisputed, pound for pound best boxer in the world, Geno felt that he was the baddest attorney on the planet. He felt that he couldn't lose. Mayhem and Geno engaged in a brief, yet intense stare down. Geno could tell that his presence was intimidating to him. The packed courtroom was filled with a deafening silence while they waited anxiously for the jury's decision. The Judge instructed everyone in the courtroom to rise to their feet. The moment of truth had arrived.

"Has the jury reached a decision?" Judge Patterson asked the jury foreman.

"Yes, we have, your Honor," he replied. The jury foreman handed the decision to the court officer, who in turn handed it to the Judge to read. Once the Judge read the verdict, it was then given to the court clerk to publish and read aloud.

"We, the jury, find the defendants, Milton and Jarvis Jackson, not guilty of all charges," the court clerk read out loud. Mayhem had to restrain himself from cursing out loud. He pounded his hand on the desk in front of him to express his anger and disappointment with the verdict. Justice had clearly not been served in his eyes.

The courtroom erupted with loud chatter. The crowd expressed a host of mixed emotions. Those individuals that supported the Jackson brothers were elated they were found not guilty. Conversely, there were just as many people there who hoped they would be sent to jail to serve a lengthy prison sentence because they had witnessed, either firsthand or through friends and family members, the destructive impact that their flooding the streets of Baltimore with heroin and cocaine had on the community as a whole.

Mayhem was livid that two heartless thugs were allowed to go free. In his opinion, they deserved to rot in jail. No matter how anyone felt about their acquittal, it was now a matter of public record and they had to accept the Court's decision. The jury felt as though there wasn't enough concrete evidence to secure a conviction of the two defendants and that was all that mattered.

"Geno, this is why we pay you the big money!" Jarvis stated ecstatically. He grabbed Geno in a bear hug and then turned toward his brother and did the same.

"You better remember that, my friend," Geno advised with a big grin on his face.

"You are the man! Geno, I don't know how you do what you do, but you make things happen!" Milton chimed in. They all erupted in laughter in the front of the courtroom. Mayhem observed their laughter and seethed with rage because he knew they were guilty and Geno's hands were just as dirty. However, he lacked the proper evidence to give them all their just due.

"Geno, where are we partying at tonight?" Milton asked. He was happy to still be a free man after he faced life in the penitentiary. He extended out his arm to shake his hand and Geno did the same in kind.

"Meet me at Maggie's at around nine o'clock tonight. I'ma have my chef prepare a feast for us to celebrate. After that, we can drink and party all night at the lounge next door, strictly VIP style. Plus, I've got a little surprise for you boys. I know you'll appreciate the gesture," Geno promised them. Maggie's was a restaurant and lounge that he owned in Little Italy. It was given to him by his father.

"That sounds like a plan. I'm down for whatever," Jarvis stated enthusiastically. He was happy to be a free man. The three of them walked out of the courtroom like old friends. Mayhem just observed them make their exit and felt disgusted. Out of the three of them, he couldn't tell who the lawyer was and who the criminals were because Geno blended in perfectly with the Jackson brothers. Mayhem swore to himself that he would use every resource in his power to bring an end to Geno's criminal empire before he retired.

Geno took his time as he walked up the street to the garage where his car was parked. When he entered the garage, the young parking attendant walked toward the entrance way to greet him. They all knew Geno by name because he always parked in the same garage whenever he had a case in the District court building on Lombard Street and he tipped them well. Plus, they saw him on the news all of the time. He was like a celebrity to them and they treated him as such.

"How are you today, Mr. Caprese?" the young attendant inquired.

"I'm good. Hey kid, what's your name?" Geno replied in return.

"It's Clarence, Mr. Caprese, but all of my friends call me Clay for short," he replied. The young man couldn't have been older than twenty-one years of age. He had an eager look of admiration in his eyes for Geno because of his wealth and his social status. He also knew about him being one of the baddest gangsters in Baltimore City.

"Well, Clay, from now on you can call me Geno. My father is Mr. Caprese. You make me feel like a senior citizen when you call me that, my friend. Do I look that old to you?" Geno asked with a serious look on his face.

"No, Sir, you don't look old at all, Mr. Caprese...umm I mean Geno," Clay replied nervously. He wanted to punch himself in the mouth because he thought he had insulted Geno. That was the last thing that he wanted to do. When Clay tried to grab Geno's keys off of the rack, he was so shook up that they slipped through his fingers and fell to the ground. Embarrassed, he bent down to pick them up.

"Relax, kid, I'm just bustin' your balls a little bit," Geno said to him while he laughed. He put his hand on his shoulder to let him know that everything was alright. Clay felt at ease and ran as fast he could up the ramp to retrieve Geno's ride. He returned a little more than two minutes later behind the wheel of Geno's Corvette. He hopped out of the car and walked toward Geno.

"Here are your keys, Geno. I made sure that nobody came near your car the whole time it was here," Clay stated in an attempt to gain favor with him.

"Thanks, kid. Here's a little something for you. Take your girlfriend out this Friday night to a fancy restaurant on me. Afterwards, make sure that she screws your brains out to show her appreciation," Geno joked. He reached into his money clip filled with nothing but one hundred dollar bills and handed him one. Clay's eyes lit up like he just hit the lottery. It was the biggest tip he ever got. He thanked Geno over and over again. Geno hopped in his ride and sped off. He left an indelible impression on Clay's young mind as he normally did with most people that crossed his path.

Chapter 5

Geno felt a rush of adrenaline jolt throughout his body when he shifted gears in his Corvette and weaved in between cars on I-95 at a speed of over one hundred miles per hour. He was a speed freak and got a rush pushing the speed limit on the open road. He just missed hitting several cars before he mashed on the brakes in the nick of time to avoid a fatal collision. He was still riding high off of his victory in court earlier in the day. He had his radio tuned to Shade 45 while Eminem's latest single blasted out of the speakers. His outward appearance was deceptive. No one would ever suspect that the seemingly mild mannered attorney with the gift of gab was a hard core rap music fan. He looked like someone who was more comfortable at the opera as opposed to backstage at a concert hanging out with the rapper Jay Z. When he was in court, he always made sure that he maintained a professional demeanor and spoke eloquently because it was necessary for him to be most effective in representing his clients. However, when he had some down time, which was rarely, he loved to put on a pair of headphones and jam to hard core gangster rap.

Geno's father, Leonardo Caprese, was sent to Baltimore from New York City in the late sixties by his mentor in the organized crime world, Lou Panelli, to take over new territory to expand his crime family. Leonardo brought his wife, Marietta, with him to start his new life. They had no children at the time and she was eager to follow him wherever he went. Leonardo was backed up by a small crew of fifteen soldiers who helped him to establish a stranglehold on all of the illegal activities that took place in the downtown Baltimore area. No money could be earned out in the streets in their territory without them receiving a cut of the action. His crew used Maggie's Restaurant, named after his mother Magdalene, as the central hub and meeting place where they conducted business.

A tall, slim handsome fellow with a witty tongue, Leonardo was considered to be one of the most dangerous killers that Baltimore had ever known. His nickname was Leo the Strangler because he loved to strangle his victims with a necktie. He didn't believe in leaving behind a bloody murder scene when he killed his victims because he was always sharply dressed and didn't want any blood to spill on his tailor made

Italian suits. He considered himself to be an upscale assassin and not a brutal killer. He also had his hands involved in several other illegal trades such as robbing armored Brinks trucks and hijacking eighteen wheelers filled with things like cigarettes and electronic goods. He ran point on several successful heists that netted him a substantial amount of money. He didn't need Social Security retirement benefits in his line of work. He created his own 401 (K) plan to be able to afford to live comfortably in his later years.

When Leonardo found out that Marietta was pregnant with Silvio, he was beyond thrilled. He was happy to have a male heir to carry on his name. Marietta was happy to play her role as the stay at home mother while Leonardo earned out in the streets. Geno came along two years later. At a young age, he and Silvio became permanent fixtures at Maggie's. All of Leonardo's crew took a liking to them. They became their play Uncles who watched over them like they were their own.

When Marietta became pregnant with Cesare eleven years after Geno, it was totally unexpected. Almost forty years old at the time, she had a rough pregnancy. She wound up delivering Cesare two months early. He was in and out of the hospital most of his early years for a host of medical issues. The family spoiled him to death. Silvio and Geno were overprotective of their little brother. The

Caprese family of five looked like a normal nuclear family on the surface, but Leonardo saw them differently. He groomed his sons to become the next generation of the Caprese crime family, but on another level.

Now in his late sixties and retired from his life of crime, Leonardo was a shell of his former self. A chronic smoker for most of his adult life, he was diagnosed with lung cancer a little over a year ago. He had numerous tell tale signs of his medical condition long before his illness was discovered, but he refused to go to the doctor because of his pride. Had he put his pride to the side and gotten treatment for his disease earlier, his doctors may have had a chance to successfully treat him, but now it was too late. His fate was inevitable and death loomed in his near future. He spent most of his time now bedridden and in and out of the hospital. He used to weigh a healthy one hundred and seventy-five pounds, but now his weight had dwindled all the way down to one hundred and forty pounds of frail flesh. He was so skinny that you could see his collarbone sticking out. When he coughed, his entire body shook violently. He didn't eat much because he had no appetite.

With his father's health getting worse every day, Geno thought about him constantly. Leonardo was his hero. He saw him as invincible and larger than life. To see him in such a weakened state had a devastating effect on him. He was frustrated because with all of the money and power that he had out in the streets and in so many other arenas, he was powerless to be able to save his father from death. He had tried every conventional medical option and every herbal form of treatment that was available to help his father, but none of them were successful. Leonardo Caprese wasn't long for this world. All Geno could do was make his father's last days as comfortable as possible. It was his job alone because his two brothers could care less about their old man.

Just as Geno was about to get off of the highway at the exit that led to his house, he saw flashing lights in his rear view mirror. He banged his hand on the steering wheel to express his anger. He knew those flashing blue and red lights from the Baltimore County police vehicles too well. He had received his share of speeding tickets throughout the years. He pulled his car over to the side of the road, turned off the car, and waited for the officer to make his way up to his vehicle. He observed him in the driver's side mirror and when he was close enough, he rolled down the window.

"Good evening officer, how's it going?" Geno asked him calmly. The officer didn't appear to be in the mood for small talk.

"Excuse me, sir; I clocked you doing ninety miles per hour in a fifty-mile per hour zone. Can I have your license and registration, please?" the officer shot back at him in a rather cold voice.

"Officer, I know I was speeding, but in my defense, I just got this baby and I wanted to test it out. So, what do you say that you just give me a warning and a little slap on the wrist? I promise you I'll do the speed limit from here on out," Geno replied jokingly. He paid no mind to the officer's request. He tried to make light of the situation, but the officer wasn't amused.

"Sir, I could take you to jail right now for reckless driving if I wanted to do so. I will ask you again, let me see your license and registration, please," the officer demanded forcefully. When he saw the officer wasn't moved by his sense of humor, Geno reached into his pants pocket to retrieve his driver's license. Next, he reached over into the glove compartment to get his vehicle registration card. He was irritated that his time was being wasted for this nonsense when he had other more important things to do. Nonetheless, he remained calm and let the officer do his job.

"Here you go, Officer," Geno stated. He reluctantly handed him the documents that he requested.

"I'll be right back," the Officer stated as he walked to his patrol car.

While he waited for the officer to return, Geno searched through his phone contacts for a phone number. When he found the one he was looking for, he pressed "Send" to place his call. He conversed for about three minutes with the person on the other end of the phone before he was interrupted by a tap on the window. The officer had returned with a ticket for him. He rolled down the window and reached his arm out to hand his phone to the officer.

"It's the Police Commissioner. He wants to speak with you for a minute."

The officer was caught totally off guard and didn't believe him. He took the phone out of Geno's hand and placed it to his ear. When Police Commissioner Leftwich confirmed that it was actually him on the phone, the officer's entire demeanor changed. He went from being a bold upholder of the law to a little child about to be scolded by his father for doing something that he had no business doing. After Commissioner Leftwich said a few choice words to him, he handed the phone back to Geno.

"I apologize for wasting your time and for the inconvenience, Mr. Caprese. I hope you enjoy the rest of your evening," he stated while he tore up the ticket he just wrote.

"You do the same, buddy, Next time you see me speeding down the road, I would advise you to look the other way because you got a pass this time, but if this happens again, I can't promise that the Commissioner will take it easy on you," Geno replied in a subtle, threatening tone. The officer didn't utter a word, but looked to be clearly shaken up by what just transpired. He walked back to his car totally humiliated and humbled. It didn't help matters for him to see Geno with a big smile on his face. He didn't even wait for the officer to get back into his car before he sped off and disappeared into traffic. His point was clearly made.

Geno had friends in high places that could make things happen for him. He loved to exert his power to get whatever he wanted. Not only was he a beast in the courtroom, but he also had powerful public officials, like Police Commissioner Leftwich and several other relevant local politicians, on his payroll. His private investigators had uncovered dirt on virtually all of them. Geno used the information he gathered freely to blackmail them into getting whatever he wanted done.

When his top private investigator, John Lucci, investigated Leftwich, he discovered that he had a thing for underage boys. He was able to hack into his home computer and he found thousands of inappropriate nude pictures of him with teenage boys stored on his hard drive. He searched through his internet browsing history and discovered that he belonged to several online groups that consisted of other sick pedophiles like himself. When Geno presented him with evidence of his dirty deeds, Leftwich pleaded with him not to expose his secret. From that moment on, he was Geno's puppet on a string. Geno used similar tactics to gain advantages in his business dealings with several top business executives to get them to invest their funds in his business ventures. He was the uncrowned King of Baltimore and felt damn proud of his position.

Chapter 6

After his little run-in with the law, Geno had to make a pit stop to check in on his wife and children to make sure that everything was okay on the home front. After he made it through the gated security entrance, he raced up the driveway to his plush mansion. It was located in the Greenspring area of Baltimore County. The estate cost him close to three million dollars to have built, but he didn't care because he wanted nothing but the best for his family. He spared no expense to make sure they had whatever they wanted or needed. The house was over seven thousand square feet and equipped with six huge bedrooms, five full sized bathrooms, an Olympic sized swimming pool with an adjacent steam room, and a host of other luxurious accommodations. He truly lived like royalty. Geno parked his Corvette in the driveway next to his Bentley coupe and Carina's Lexus truck. He got out of his car and walked toward the front door. When he stepped inside, he was greeted by the family pet, Gabriel. He was a two year old bull terrier that Geno purchased for his kids when he was just a puppy. He wanted his children to have the experience of growing up with a pet because he always wanted a dog when he was a child, but his father would never get him one.

"Hey, boy, did you miss me?" Geno asked him playfully while he rubbed his head. Gabriel responded by pawing at his pants leg.

"He sure did miss you and so did his Mommy," Carina chimed in while she stood at the top of the stairs. She happened to be walking down the hallway when she heard Geno enter the residence. Carina's beauty was unmatched. She had long, jet black hair that complemented her light brown eyes and bronze colored complexion. Her slender, yet shapely figure remained intact even after she had two children. She was dressed in a pair of low rise jeans and a t-shirt.

"Come show me how much you missed me then," Geno challenged her. No sooner than he spoke, she ran down the stairs and jumped into his arms. She kissed him on his lips gently. Geno returned her affection by playfully smacking her backside.

Even though she just saw him earlier in the day, every moment they were apart seemed like an eternity to Carina. She loved Geno with every ounce of her heart and soul and he felt the same way. It was her life's mission to be his wife and to be the mother of his children. From the very first moment she saw him walk into the men's clothing store she worked in many years ago, she fantasized that she would one day marry him. Geno used to shop at the store regularly and Carina caught him checking her out on several occasions. When he finally asked her out on a date, all of her dreams came true.

Due to his magnetic aura and charm, the chemistry between them developed instantly. Geno was in his second year of law school at the time and had dreams of becoming a big time attorney in the future. She wanted to help him fulfill his dream. At the time, she had no clue he lived a double life or that he was in a relationship with another woman. When she found out about Amy, as well as his illegal activities, it was too late. She was already head over heels in love with Geno.

Carina accepted Geno for who he was because she believed that they were destined to be together. No other woman or the law could stand in their way. Geno loved the fact that she didn't judge him like Amy did. Amy always tried to get him to change his ways and live what he called a square lifestyle. Geno valued his education, but he never gave up his ties to the streets because that was his foundation. Amy's inability to be spontaneous was one of the primary reasons that he chose to break things off with her and to be with Carina. He also didn't have to explain himself to Carina because she was just as adventurous and she understood that he had to be who he felt he was born to be.

While Amy had plans to be an attorney herself, Carina had no problem being a stay at home mom. She was the perfect fit for his lifestyle. She loved him for being the brilliant attorney that he was just as much as she respected his gangster side. She never judged him or asked questions about his illegal activities because it was none of her business. She had his back for better or worse and whatever he wanted her to know, Geno had no problem telling her. Geno loved his family more than anything else in the world and would die or kill for them without a second thought.

"I think we need to take this into the bedroom. What do you say?" Geno suggested with his hands wrapped around her waist.

"I think you need to behave because your children might come down here any minute. We can continue this later on tonight," Carina advised.

"I'ma hold you to that, my love," Geno promised her while they embraced each other at the front door. With all of the aggression he showed in the courtroom, he was a teddy bear at home with Carina and his kids. They were his sole source of peace and comfort. Geno and Carina walked hand in hand up the spiraling staircase so they could check in on their children. Geno's day wasn't complete without spending a few moments with them.

Stefan was eight years old and the spitting image of Geno. He stayed up under his father every chance that he got. Geno felt proud to have a miniature version of him walking around the Earth. It guaranteed him that his name would live on for generations to come. He bragged about him every chance he got. When he peaked in his room, he observed him doing his homework. Stefan was a straight A student in school and all of his teachers raved about how intelligent he was. Geno planned to stay on top of him to make sure he stayed focused on his studies so that he would one day surpass his accomplishments in life.

"Hey what's up, slugger?" Geno uttered. Stefan stopped what he was doing when he saw Geno. He got up from his desk and ran toward his father to give him a hug. Geno picked him up in his arms.

"Hey, Daddy, guess what? I got an "A" on my test in Math class," Stefan said proudly. He walked over to his desk and retrieved the test paper to show it to Geno.

"That's my lil' man and Daddy is so proud of you. Here is something for you. Get your

Mommy to take you out to buy a game or something," Geno said. He reached in his pocket and pulled out a C note and gave it to Stefan.

"Thanks, Daddy. You're the best!" Stefan said excitedly. He gave him another hug. His young mind raced with ideas of what he could buy with the money. Images of a video game, candy, and a host of other little treats ran through his head.

"Geno, that's too much money for an eight year old boy to have. Stop spoiling him so much," Carina butted in. Even though they were financially well off, Carina didn't want their children to feel too privileged and unable to understand the concept of hard work to obtain success in life. She and Geno argued about this constantly, but she usually gave in and let him have his way. He was the King of the castle and always got the last word.

"Awww, come on, babes, he needs to learn how to handle money at some point and time so why not start him out young? Besides, his Daddy is a rich man and he can afford to splurge on his little man if he is doing so well in school," he reasoned. Carina just smiled and didn't say another word. Geno talked with Stefan for a few more minutes before he let him get back to his homework.

When he walked down the hall to Gianna's room, the atmosphere was totally different. Her room was a mess. There were clothes all over the floor. Gianna had dirty dishes and candy wrappers on her dresser. She sat down on her bed with her Beats by Dre headphones on listening to music. She was unfazed by the clutter that surrounded her. While Stefan excelled in school, Gianna struggled to get C's in her classes. It wasn't because she wasn't smart enough to do the work, but she just didn't apply herself. No matter how many times Geno or Carina got on her for not doing better with her schoolwork, nothing changed. Her mind was elsewhere.

Gianna had it set in her mind from the time she was eight years old that she wanted to either be a model or fashion designer. Her stunning good looks that she inherited from Carina made her chances a realistic possibility. She had Geno's stubborn and highly self-motivated personality which made taking "NO" for an answer something that would never happen. Her walls were filled with pictures of all of the supermodels that she idolized. Seeing that being hard on her didn't work, Geno and Carina decided to change their approach with Gianna. They encouraged her interest in fashion and modeling by enrolling her in a teenage model training program that Carina found online.

The program was located in Washington, D.C., and Carina took Gianna there for their weekly meetings on Saturdays. Since she enrolled in the program, her grades in school improved slightly to the point that she was now a B level student. It wasn't what Geno expected from her, but any progress was better than none he reasoned. Either way, she was his first born and his baby girl. He would support her one hundred percent with whatever she wanted to do in life.

"Hey, big head, you didn't hear me calling you? I guess you don't have time for your old man, huh?" he asked. When she didn't respond to him calling her name several times, he crept up behind her and took her headphones off of her ears. His actions startled her. When she saw that it was Geno, she jumped up and gave him a big hug.

"Hey, Big G, what's happening? I was in here listening to Eminem's new CD. It's hot," she replied. She didn't call him Daddy or Pops like most teenagers referred to their father. He was big "G" and she was little "G". Geno gave her permission to call him that even though Carina didn't like it at all. She wanted him to act more like her father than her friend, but Geno paid her no mind. He wanted the same kind of open relationship with his kids that he had with his father growing up. He didn't want to be the iron fisted dictator type of parent, but instead felt comfortable being looked at as the cool Dad his children could talk to about anything that was on their minds.

"Yeah, it is pretty dope. I was just blasting it in my car on the ride home. On another note, did you do your homework?" he asked. To have a father that used hip slang words like "dope" or "fly" made Gianna feel like she had the coolest, down to earth father in the world. She bragged about him to her friends all of the time.

"Yes, I did. Here it is right here," she replied. She lifted her notebook off of the bed and showed him her completed assignments.

"That's what I'm talking about! That's Daddy's princess. You're a Caprese. We get things done," he said with pride. Carina just observed their interaction without saying a word. She wished that she had as close of a bond with her children as Geno did. However, the same charm and wit that he won her over with was just as appealing to his children as opposed to her efforts to be the strict mother figure she felt they needed in their lives to grow up and become productive members of society. Even though she wasn't as cool as Geno, she and Gianna were able to bond whenever they went shopping or to the nail or hair salon. She truly appreciated their girlie time together.

"Hey, Big G, check out my newest modeling pictures. Tell me what you think," Gianna requested. She pulled out her portfolio so that he could see her photos.

"Sweetie, you look like a million bucks. Your old man is gonna have to keep a closer eye on you so that none of these young punks tries to steal your heart," Geno joked, but he was dead serious. He couldn't believe how fast his little girl was growing up in front of his eyes. She was almost at the age that she would start to have an interest in boys, if she hadn't already started. He wasn't prepared for that stage in her life at all. He envisioned himself as the kind of father who would be at the front door with a shotgun locked, loaded, and ready to shoot whenever some young man wanted to take his baby girl out on a date.

"Thanks, Big G. You're the best," Gianna replied with a big smile on her face. She loved to receive his approval.

They talked for a few more minutes before the conversation was cut short when Gianna received a text message from her best friend, Pia. Geno and Carina exited her room so she could have girl talk in private. While they walked down the hallway toward their bedroom, Geno grabbed Carina by her arm and pulled her into one of their spare bedrooms. He shut the door behind them and made sure that it was locked. Carina was totally caught off guard, but turned on at the same time.

"Mr. Caprese, what is that naughty mind of yours up to now?" Carina inquired.

"Forget what I said earlier. I can't wait until tonight. I need a taste of that sweet thing right now. The kids are occupied and it's just me and you in this room alone. I'm in the mood for a quickie," Geno replied rather directly and to the point.

Before Carina had a chance to respond, Geno undid her pants and let them fall down to her ankles. He did the same with her panties. He undid his trousers and let them drop to the floor as well. Carina salivated at the site of his stiff manhood when it poked out of his boxer shorts. Geno inserted himself inside of her to enjoy her sweetness. Every time he was inside of her, it felt like the first time. He never grew tired of making love to Carina.

"Geno Caprese, you are such a bad boy, but you're my bad boy. Give it to me, baby!" Carina pleaded in a low whisper.

Geno gave Carina just what she desired. It was spontaneous quickies like this that kept the flames of romance alive in their relationship. When Geno entered her, his penis made her feel so alive inside that she wanted to moan out loud to voice her feelings of sheer delight, but she didn't want the children to hear them. Instead, she just closed her eyes and braced herself on the dresser with her hands while Geno had his way with her body.

Chapter 7

Geno's eyes were pleased by what he saw when he pulled up to Maggie's and parked in his reserved parking spot in front of the establishment. There were several small groups of individuals outside of the restaurant waiting to be seated so that they could feast on some of the finest Italian dishes offered in the city of Baltimore. When he looked to his right, he could see through the glass front window all of the people crammed inside of the lounge for happy hour. The place was filled with college students, business men and women, and gangsters. They were all there for the same reason-to have a good time. As long as they kept ordering drinks, the bartenders would keep pouring them, and Geno's money would continue to multiply. There was nothing sweeter than the sound of his money machine when he counted up his profits at the end of the week. Geno had shed his suit from earlier in the day and was now dressed casually in a pair of slacks and a Polo sweater. He got out of his car and proceeded to walk toward the front door.

"Hey, Geno, it's good to see you. Business is good tonight at both spots. Your brothers just arrived a little while earlier. They're in the restaurant waiting on you along with those two Black soul brothers," Carlo, the door man stated with a slight bit of disdain in his voice. It was clear that he was a racist and didn't care for Black folks too much. Geno knew this very well, but he didn't care. Milton and Jarvis were his guests and they were to be treated with the same respect as any other guests that visited his establishment.

"That's what I like to hear, Uncle Carlo. Keep an eye on my ride and make sure that nobody touches her. I just got her cleaned the other day," Geno instructed him. He glanced at his ride and admired the bright shine that reflected off of the hood from the street lights.

"I sure will," Carlo replied. Geno walked past him toward the front door of the restaurant. He smiled and spoke to several of the patrons along the way.

Carlo was an older Italian gentleman, in his late sixties, who walked with a limp from being shot in the leg many years ago. He was an associate of Geno's father from back in the days when he was a force to be reckoned with in the streets. Geno called him Uncle Carlo because he was like family. Carlo used to be a top earner in the streets for years until the government shut him down and sent him to prison for almost eleven years for a botched bank robbery. He had also served time for charges such as running a whore house, possession of a handgun, and armed robbery.

Geno was fresh out of law school when he represented him for the bank robbery charge, but was able to get him a reduced sentence compared to the forty years that the prosecutor had tried to offer him in the first plea deal. Even though Carlo couldn't afford his legal fees, he helped him on the strength of his ties to his father. When he was released from jail, he returned home broke because the government seized all of his assets. With his health failing after he suffered a heart attack while incarcerated, Geno felt obligated to help him which was why he worked at Maggie's. No matter how much legal money he made, Geno remained loyal to the streets and his creed. His father always taught him to be an honorable man and to look out for old school gangsters from their circle when they fell on hard times and couldn't earn anymore. Geno was an obedient son and always took heed to his father's wise advice.

Once he was inside the restaurant, Geno walked toward the back, in the direction of the large dining area that was sectioned off to be used for large private parties. He called the restaurant earlier in the day and spoke with the head chef to arrange for a special Italian feast to be prepared for Jarvis and Milton as a celebration of their acquittal on all charges. The Jackson brothers were more than just his clients. They were a part of his crime family. They made Geno a significant amount of money over the years so it was in his best interest to make sure they stayed on the streets. When he walked into the room, everyone had already started eating without him. He was late because of his little romantic tryst with Carina.

"I see you hogs couldn't wait on me, huh? Look at you all. You're just a bunch of savages," Geno joked as he scanned the room and saw them all with healthy plates of food in front of them. They all burst out in laughter. Seated at his table were Silvio and Cesare, the Jackson brothers, and his two partners in crime since elementary school, Cappi and Sal. Rome and Dre, two of the Jackson brothers' top lieutenants, and several of their other crew members were seated at adjacent tables.

"Yo, what up Geno, what's shaking?" Cesare asked in his high pitched voice. He was dressed in a royal blue Sean John sweatshirt with several gold chains around his neck.

In his mid twenties, Cesare's life was totally off track. He was the loose cannon in the family. He loved to smoke marijuana and party hard all of the time. He had big dreams of becoming a rap superstar one day, but that would never happen because he lacked the most essential element-talent. Standing five feet and nine inches tall with a muscular build, he had the good looks to be a rap superstar, but his rap skills sucked. He surrounded himself with yes men who boosted his ego and led him to believe that he had a shot at success in the entertainment industry.

Cesare, who went by the rap moniker Chilly C, was determined to see himself on MTV or VH1 someday. He was a superstar in his own mind, but the rest of the world viewed him as a joke. The only reason why nobody told him that he wasn't good was because he was Geno and Silvio's little baby brother and they feared their reaction.

Throughout the years, Cesare caught several petty drug possession and assault charges that Geno had to waste his time in court representing him to make sure he stayed out on the streets. After his last arrest two years ago for beating up his on again and off again girlfriend, Princess, Geno had enough of his immature antics. When he paid Princess off not to come to court to testify against Cesare, he gave Cesare a stern warning that this was the last time he would bail him out of a jam. He told him that if he didn't get his life together, he would cut him off and leave him to fend for himself.

Cesare took heed to Geno's warning and started to get his life together. Even though he still liked to smoke weed and drink alcohol, he decided to come to work for the family business. Geno made him the assistant manager at Lila's, a strip club the family owned, which was located on the infamous Block in downtown Baltimore. His good friend, Cappi, was the manager and he took Cesare under his wing to show him the ropes. Geno hoped that Cesare would learn some business skills from Cappi that might eventually convince him to let go of his fledgling rap career and dedicate himself to the family business.

"Hey little bro, who do you think you are Vanilla Ice? Sil, look at this guy, he's something else I tell you," Geno joked. He walked over to Cesare and gave him a hug. Cesare wasn't amused by his statement, but felt offended.

"Come on, son, why are you trying to play me like that? Respect my swag, big bro. My gangster is official," Cesare shot back at him. He moved his arms and hands to further emphasize his point. Milton and Jarvis found his little routine to be amusing and called him a wigga behind his back. To see a white boy like Cesare imitate the lifestyle and culture of a young Black male from the inner city was insulting, but they never said a word about it to Geno. They tolerated Cesare because he was Geno's little brother and they did good business together.

"You call that swag? I call it clownin', but hey what do I now? It's your world, lil' bro,"

Geno stated dismissively. His attention was focused on the magnificent buffet his chefs prepared. He was starving.

"Hey, Geno, take it easy on lil' bro. He might surprise us and make more money than the two of us combined one day. Everybody's not a stuffed suit kinda guy like you," Silvio rebutted in a joking manner, but he was dead serious. He was around the same height as Geno, but a little thicker with dark wavy hair. He always took up for Cesare whenever Geno talked down to him. Geno refused to acknowledge Silvio's comment. Silvio took his demeanor as being disrespectful, but Geno could care less. He was the boss of the Caprese family. He proceeded to engage in conversation with Jarvis Jackson.

Silvio was the oldest of the Caprese boys by two years, but Geno was the smartest and most loved and respected of the brothers in their Little Italy neighborhood growing up. He always got the best looking girls and excelled in both football and wrestling when they were in high school. While Geno went on to graduate from college and to become a well respected attorney, Silvio dropped out of high school in his final year to dive right into the street life. He thought his father would be proud of his decision to continue his legacy by following in his footsteps, but Leonardo was livid about Silvio's decision.

Even though he was a hard core street thug, Leonardo understood how the culture of the gangster life had changed on many levels. While shy locking, committing robberies, and prostitution were still good avenues to earn in the underworld, Leonardo saw the potential for his sons to earn even more money if they took some of their dirty money and infiltrated the corporate world by setting up legitimate businesses. He wanted his sons to go to college and learn everything they could that would be beneficial to the family business to take it to the next level. The only one of his sons that understood his vision was Geno.

Silvio hated the fact their father had a closer relationship with Geno than he did with him and Cesare. He felt he should be his father's favorite son because he was his first born. However, Leonardo saw the leadership potential Geno had to carry on the family business whereas Silvio was more equipped to be a street level enforcer or worker. Geno had the polished look and mannerisms to be the face of the Caprese family to the legitimate world. Silvio was the one who did the dirty work and handled the day to day operations on the streets. They loved each other as brothers, but it was obvious that there was tension there.

Geno did his best to get along with his brother, but Silvio's heart was filled with deep-seated envy that came to the surface every now and then. Silvio had never gotten over the way

Geno cleverly wrestled control of their crew that he started from up under his nose. He felt that he should rightfully be in charge, but in reality, he didn't have what it took to be the Boss. He lacked the charisma, business savvy, and ability to make the right decisions that benefited their entire team like Geno did. Over time, the facts spoke for themselves. Geno was clearly the man for the job.

"I'm just bustin' your balls, lil bro. You know I love you, kid. Anyway, tonight is about my good friends, Milton and Jarvis. Let's toss one back for them to celebrate their freedom. Salute to you two soldiers for being stand up men and not rats like some of these heartless bastards who claim to be about this life of ours," Geno stated emphatically to express his disdain for government informants. He hated a snitch more than anything else in the world because loyalty was as important as breathing to him. If you had no loyalty to your family and crew, then you were the lowest form of scum to Geno and worthy of death.

Geno sat down at the head of the table and grabbed the bottle of Dom Perignon that was positioned in front of him. He poured himself a glass. When he planned the dinner, he made sure that all of his guests had their own bottle to drink along with their meal. They all followed his lead and pour themselves a glass of champagne as well. Geno did everything with style and class. To him, it was the only way to be. He was a gentleman and a gangster, well equipped to do business in both worlds.

"Cheers," the Jackson brothers said in unison while they raised their glasses in the air.

Everybody at the table tipped their glasses and gulped down the champagne. With the toast out of the way, everybody got back to devouring the delicious food and washed it down with the rest of their bottles of Dom Perignon. It was a festive occasion for all to celebrate.

Chapter 8

As the night of celebration wore on, everybody was stuffed from the good food, inebriated from all of the alcohol, and in a cheerful mood. Geno decided to move the party over to the lounge next door. He had the VIP section roped off to separate them from the regular partygoers. A gang of beautiful women vied to join them in the exclusive section of the lounge because the way they were all dressed, it was clear they all had money. Everybody handpicked the women that they wanted to entertain them for the night, with the exception of Geno. He didn't cheat on his wife anymore because he learned a valuable lesson a few years ago when Carina found out about an affair that he had with a young lady named Sherita.

Sherita was a young, African American female who used to be his personal assistant. She was sexy in every sense of the word and just as crazy mentally. She and Geno had a hot and heavy affair for several months before he decided to cut it off because she became obsessed with him. She would call his phone constantly, at all hours of the night, and leave him sexually suggestive messages.

Geno wound up firing her, but Sherita still continued to stalk him. When Carina heard one of her steamy messages and saw the naked pictures that she sent to Geno in text messages, she was so incensed that she threatened to leave him and take their kids with her. It took Geno months of wooing Carina with gifts and affection before she forgave him. After that fiasco, he realized that his life was incomplete without Carina in it and no woman was worth losing his family. Sherita picked the wrong man to harass. Geno was forced to make her disappear without a trace at the hands of one of his skilled assassins for hire. That experience was a life lesson well learned. Carina was the only woman he needed.

Geno just sat back and observed his crew having a good time and lived vicariously through them. He had his share of women in his youth to last him a lifetime. His mind was more focused today on the next business power move he could make. To pull off a corporate takeover or to close out a million dollar deal gave him a rush that was better than sex. He sipped on a glass of Courvoisier and smoked on a Montecristo cigar. He was content as could be.

He had no worries whatsoever. Maggie's was packed to capacity and that meant more money for him. He bobbed his head to the music while he reclined on the plush sofa. Jarvis got up from his seat and walked over to where he was seated.

"Hey, Geno, where's the surprise that you said you had for us?" Jarvis asked him.

"Ahhh, yes, it almost slipped my mind. Go get your brother and follow me down to my office," Geno replied calmly. He made eye contact with Silvio and motioned with his head to indicate that he wanted him to join them as well. Silvio pushed the pretty young blonde off of his lap and got up out of his seat to join Geno and the Jackson brothers in Geno's office.

Jarvis walked back over to the other side of the VIP section and whispered in Milton's ear for him to join him in Geno's office. They all walked out of the VIP section to the back of the lounge and toward the rear door that led to Geno's office. Two burly security guards were posted outside at all times. No one was to enter Geno's office without his permission. If anybody tried, there would be fatal repercussions.

When they reached Geno's office and walked inside, Milton and Jarvis were surprised at what they saw. Big P was tied down to a chair in the center of the room with his mouth gagged. Geno had two of his goons watch over him to make sure that he didn't try to escape. They sat back on the large sofa and watched him squirm and wiggle about in the chair in an attempt to get free. No matter how hard he tried, he wasn't going anywhere. When he saw Milton and Jarvis, he urinated on himself. Big P knew that things were about to go from bad to worse.

"Geno, how the hell did you find this fool? When you said that he gave the Feds the slip, I was sure that he had left the country," Milton stated to express his shock.

"I've told you several times before, nothing goes down in this city without me knowing. I'm the real Mayor of Baltimore City. I couldn't let this filthy pig get away with betraying my good business associates. What kind of man would I be to let that go down, huh? This is my gift to you and a small way for me to show my appreciation for all of the money you've made me over the years. Don't ask questions, just say thank you, my brother," Geno advised him.

He never ceased to amaze the Jackson brothers. Geno always found a way to make things happen. He was beyond resourceful. How he was able to steal a federal witness out of custody was beyond their comprehension. They didn't want to know. The bottom line was that Geno delivered a gift to them which was immeasurable in monetary value. They both just nodded their heads in Geno's direction to express their gratitude and then turned their attention to their former associate. Jarvis walked over to him and removed the gag from his mouth.

"What's up, P? I bet you never thought you would see us again, huh?" Jarvis asked with pure rage in his voice. Before he could respond, he punched him in the face several times. Milton joined in on the party and began to rain down on him with blow after blow until his arms got tired. The impact of his blows caused Big P and the chair he was in to fall to the floor. The wooden chair broke into pieces due to Big P's body weight. They both took a break to get a second wind. Big P, covered in his own blood, took his brief respite as an opportunity to try and plead his case.

"Please don't kill me! I had no choice! My back was against the wall! They threatened to put my mother in jail! You've gotta forgive me! We go back too far! I'm not ready to die!" Big P begged for his life.

As it turned out, Big P had opened up a barber shop and purchased a few properties in his mother's name with drug money. During their investigation, the Feds combed through all of her financial assets and knew that she couldn't afford to purchase the business and the homes on her school teacher salary. Big P agreed to give up Milton and Jarvis after he was arrested in exchange for the Feds not pursuing a case against his mother.

"You're right, P, we do go back a long ways. We all used to be out in the traps grinding in East Baltimore until the wee hours of the morning getting that money, but you seem to have forgotten about those times. You forgot about the most important thing in this life of ours and that's loyalty. We've always had your back and gave you anything you ever wanted and you repaid us by selling us out? We've got the best lawyer in this city on our team and you could've beaten the case, but you chose the sucker route to become a rat," Milton methodically broke down his betrayal to him. He wanted him to fully understand why he was about to die and to think about it every second until he took his last breath. Feeling a burst of energy, he kicked Big P several times in the rib area as his body was sprawled out on the ground. Big P winced in pain.

"I'm sorry, Milton! I'm sorry, man. Please let me go. I swear I'll go away and you'll never hear from or see me again," Big P continued to beg.

"You're right, homey, because where you're about to go, men don't talk," Jarvis butted in.

The sight of a disloyal bastard like Big P made his stomach turn. The longer he was left alive to breathe, the more time he would be reminded about his disloyalty. Add in all of the liquor that he had consumed as additional motivation, Jarvis had decided that it was time for this little game to end. He pulled out his gun from around his waistline and proceeded to bash in Big P's skull with the butt of his weapon. Milton took out his knife and cut out Big P's tongue. There was blood everywhere.

Luckily, Geno had his boys line the floor area with a sheet of plastic so that none of Big P's blood would spill out onto his expensive carpet. No one could hear Big P's cries and screams for mercy because the music upstairs muffled out the sound. Geno sat behind his desk and watched the vicious beating that Milton and Jarvis put on Big P while he puffed on a cigar. He loved the sight of blood and to see a snake like Big P suffer for his actions. Silvio enjoyed the show as well. Geno's two burly goons were there not only to watch over Big P, but to also dispose of the body once the Jackson brothers were done torturing him. Milton and Jarvis toyed with Big P for several more minutes before they realized he had stopped breathing. Now that he was dead, they could rest easy because he was no longer a threat. There was now one less rat in the world. They could resume business as usual, moving major weight without interference.

Chapter 9

Cesare always left from being around Geno in a bad mood. Nothing he ever did was good enough to please his older brother. He felt like all Geno ever did was judge him and treat him like he was stupid. He didn't support his music career because he saw it as a waste of time. Geno wanted his little brother to become a suit and tie businessman like him, but that wasn't Cesare's style. He liked to be in the streets in the thick of the limelight and the hustle. That was why he and Silvio got along so well. They both were comfortable being in the streets whereas Geno had changed from how he used to be. Now, he liked to sit behind a desk all day and give out orders like a big time executive as though his hands weren't as dirty as theirs were. He liked the fact Silvio talked to him and not at him like Geno did. He didn't judge him, but supported his aspirations.

"I need to get my mind right, Rah. Every time I'm around Geno he throws me off my game. My brother is an asshole," Cesare explained to his best friend, Rah, as he reminisced about their encounter from the night before.

"You focus on the wrong things, C. You worry too much about what your brother thinks of you instead of just not giving a damn about his opinion. You should just let him talk and let his words go in one ear and right out of the other," Rah advised him.

"That's easier said than done. My brother has a way of making you do things against your will. He didn't get to be the powerful man that he is by accident," Cesare shot back. If he tried to ignore Geno, things would only get worse. Geno acted more like his father than Leonardo did in his currently weakened state. Everything he did always managed to get back to Geno somehow. He had eyes and ears everywhere it seemed.

Rah and Cesare were seated inside of his Range Rover truck parked in front of Lila's. Cesare was due at work two hours ago, but he was otherwise occupied sexing one of his many side chicks. Cappi had called his phone several times, but he refused to answer. He knew he would be pissed off he was late for work, but he didn't care. There was nothing he could do to him because he worked for Geno and Cesare was his little brother. Cappi knew not to cross the line with him because the last thing that he wanted to do was to feel Geno's wrath. Even though Geno criticized him all of the time for his bad life decisions, Cesare was still family and he protected him as such. Cesare motioned for Rah to pass him the blunt that he now had in his mouth. Rah obliged his request.

"C, you just wanted to taste some of this good smoke, Mon. Don't blame that on Geno stressing you out. You would be high if you didn't see him last night. Ain't no need to front for me, brother. Me know how you do," Rah replied in his thick Jamaican accent. He was half choking and half laughing at his partner in crime. Cesare had to laugh as well because Rah spoke the truth. He smoked weed all day and all night. He couldn't remember the last time he went a day without inhaling bud since he first fell in love with it in middle school. Geno hated the fact that he got high because it went against the code that their father taught them that a true wise guy didn't indulge in drug use.

"Yeah, you're right, homey. This exotic Golden Jamaican Kush gets me in my zone," Cesare confessed. He took a few more totes from the blunt. The radio inside of the truck blasted one of the cuts from Cesare's rap mixtape. He bobbed his head to the beat of the track. He was so high that it didn't matter that his lyrics weren't in tune with the music. In his mind, nobody could see him on the microphone.

Rah, whose government name was Ezekiel Clarke, was Cesare's best friend since they met in high school. Rah had just moved to the United States from Jamaica. His long dreadlocks and Caribbean accent stuck out like a sore thumb at their virtually all White Catholic school. There were a few other Black students at the school, but none of them had Rah's high level of self-confidence to be able to blend in as comfortably as he did amongst his White counterparts. In fact, many of the White kids were intrigued by his thick Jamaican accent and the stories he would share with them about his life back in his homeland. A tall, dark skinned brother with an athletic build, he had his fair share of sexual experiences with several Caucasian females who were eager to get to know the mysterious and handsome brother from the Caribbean.

Rah came from a die-hard Rastafarian family. He wore long dreadlocks as a tribute to his proud heritage. His father, Nesta, was a well-known, politically connected businessman in his hometown of Kingston. He also was just as notorious for being an international ganja smuggler. He was arrested and charged with having a man that owed him a large drug debt murdered, but he beat the charge by paying off the corrupt judge and bribing several jury members.

After his brush with the law, Nesta decided to move his family to the United States. He set up shop in Miami, Florida, and continued his drug operation trafficking marijuana up and down the East Coast. Over time, Nesta relocated his family to Baltimore because he decided to merge his drug organization with his cousin Liddell's cocaine ring that he had in place in the city. He surmised they could make far more money united than as two separate entities. Nesta's assessment was dead on point. Since they merged their posses, they had a stranglehold on the marijuana and cocaine trade in West Baltimore. Their primary rivals in the drug game were the Jackson brothers, who controlled all of the East side of town. Over the years, they engaged in several battles over turf, with neither side giving an inch.

Over time, Rah became his father's right hand man and the heir to the throne. Nesta schooled Rah on the ins and outs of the drug game and Rah was an attentive student. He soaked up the knowledge Nesta imparted onto him like a sponge. Even though his father was a drug dealer and wanted him to follow in his footsteps, Nesta made sure that Rah went to the best schools that America had to offer. Like Leonardo tried to do with Geno and his brothers, Nesta wanted to teach Rah the art of being the gentleman gangster. He wanted him to be the kind of educated thug who could blend in with the legitimate business men of the world. He wanted him to be able to speak their language and use his illegally gained financial resources to cleverly make the American free market economic system work to his advantage. To have a strong financial stake in corporate America would only strengthen their position of power in the underworld and make them virtually untouchable by law enforcement. Rah took heed to his lessons and remained a straight A student throughout high school. He went on to graduate from Morgan State University with a Bachelor's degree in Journalism and a minor in African Studies.

After graduating from college, Rah now ran a successful underground magazine called *Voice of the Wretched*, which centered its stories around the plight of oppressed members of the African diaspora from all walks of life. His magazine featured the stories of individuals who were political prisoners, incarcerated drug kingpins, leaders of revolutionary movements in Third World countries, and a host of others who felt that their voice needed to be heard. With his father's financial backing and international political connections, he and his staff of writers were able to gain access to a host of controversial figures to interview. The magazine had a steady circulation in the hundreds of thousands internationally and generated significant legitimate income for Rah. It was the perfect cover. He also ran a culture arts store that sold Afrocentric and Jamaican art work, health and beauty supplies specifically for people of color, incense, and body oils.

Rah's sharp business mind and pride in his Jamaican heritage made it hard for most to understand the connection that he shared with Cesare. However, in addition to his educational and business interests, he also had a strong love for rap music just like Cesare did. That was how they first connected with each other. His favorite rap artists were Jay Z, Nas, 50 Cent, and Kendrick Lamar while Cesare was a Notorious B.I.G. and E-40 fan. He and Cesare used to go back and forth about who was the best rapper all of the time in school. Plus, they also both loved to smoke weed religiously. In addition to those things in common, Rah felt sympathy for Cesare growing up in the shadow of his father and Geno's larger than life personalities because he experienced the same thing as his father's heir apparent. The difference between the two was that Rah embraced the challenge whereas Cesare sought to escape the responsibility at every turn.

When Rah's father found out who Cesare's brother was, he instantly used their relationship to his advantage. Nesta wasted no time in getting Rah to persuade Cesare to attempt to arrange a meeting between him and Geno so that they could discuss mutually beneficial business. Initially, Geno wasn't receptive to the idea because he knew the notorious reputation of excessive violence that was associated with Jamaican posses. The brutal murders that they committed were bad for his clean cut image. He also had second thoughts about doing business with him because of his relationship with the Jackson brothers. He didn't want to step on their toes by doing business with him. However, when he finally agreed to a sit down meeting with Nesta, he was genuinely impressed with his business presentation, but he was still leery of him. Geno always took his time and was careful when he decided to let someone into his business circle. Nesta seemed a bit too ambitious to be a member of his team.

When Nesta broke down the cheap wholesale prices he could offer Geno on hundreds of pounds of marijuana at a time, the profit margin he stood to make from their relationship made it make perfect sense to him. In response to Nesta's business proposition, Geno agreed to beat the prices Nesta and Liddell paid their plug for cocaine and heroin. They also had to agree to not make any further attempts to expand their business into the Jackson brothers' territory. Nesta agreed to the peace treaty because the money he and Liddell could make made the situation make perfect business sense. Thus far, their relationship had been a success because they both made millions of dollars from their arrangement and there was peace between the two rival factions.

Outside of the drug business, Nesta had managed to build a solid legitimate portfolio of his own, but it was nowhere near the level of Geno's operation. He owned several Jamaican restaurants and nightclubs in Baltimore City and

Prince Georges County, two areas with a nice sized Caribbean population. He also owned a travel agency that did well. To expand his corporation, Nesta made several attempts to get Geno to include him in on his legal business ventures, but Geno turned him down flat every time. Geno respected Nesta, but he didn't trust him enough to let him into that part of his inner circle. Nesta took his rejection as disrespectful, like any Boss would, but he held his peace. He saw no reason to mess up the good business partnership they currently had. When the time was right, he was sure that he would be able to persuade Geno to see things his way and agree to let him in on the real money.

"Girl, what do you want? You've been ringing my phone all day. I'll be home when I get there!" Cesare yelled into the phone at Princess, his on and off again live-in girlfriend. She didn't even get a chance to respond before he hung up. As soon as he ended the call, she called right back, but he let the call go to voicemail. She did the same thing at least ten more times before she finally gave up. This was their normal routine in their drama filled relationship.

"C, you need to treat your lady with more respect than you do. You know she loves you like crazy, Mon. You have to treat the lady like a queen and she won't hound you so much, you feel me?" Rah advised him.

"Rah, she's a damn nuisance. If she didn't have that bangin' body, I would have been left her alone," Cesare joked. Ever since he was in high school, he dated Black females exclusively. A white girl with a flat butt could do nothing for him. He liked his women with a lot of junk in their trunk that jiggled when they walked.

"You Yankee boys love the sweet nectar of the Black woman, but can't deal with her passion and spirit that make up her beautiful essence," Rah stated with wisdom beyond his years about the obsession many Caucasian males had with the Black woman's shapely physical attributes but their inability to appreciate her inner beauty.

"Whatever, Mr. Professor. I ain't in the mood for you to be kicking knowledge to me right now about the value of my Nubian queen. Besides, with all of them queens that you have on a string with your smooth talking ass, you have no room to judge me, brother. I know a lot of them would probably cut your dick off if they knew how much you loved to mess around with them blonde haired beach bunnies," Cesare jabbed at him.

"What can I say, my brother? I love them all. I need me a variety of women in my life. I love girls, girls, girls," Rah sung mimicking Jay Z's song by the same name. He was just as guilty as Cesare of being a womanizer. The two good friends had to laugh at each other. They went back and forth all of the time about their drama filled escapades with the many women in their lives.

"Yes indeed, playboy. A man can never get enough of some good punany. Man, this weed is proper, Rah. It has me feeling righteous. Bump that club. I don't feel like working tonight. I need to head over to the studio to lay down this track while my mind is open right now," Cesare suggested. He and Rah had put their money together to open up a recording studio in downtown Baltimore. They rented out blocks of studio time to up and coming local recording artists to generate additional income for themselves.

"Let's get to it then, my brother," Rah stated.

He drove his truck en route to the studio and was forced to be tortured by the sound of Cesare's horrible rap songs the whole ride there. He knew that Cesare sucked as a rapper and had no chance in hell to make it in the music business, but he nonetheless, encouraged his pipe dream. As long as he had a good relationship with him and his father and Geno remained on good terms making major money together, then it made perfect sense to let his good friend, Cesare, live in his fantasy world. It was a small price to pay for maintaining the good life that he lived.

Chapter 10

Why do I have to baby sit this asshole? Damn, I wish I could whack this lame ass loser. He's nothing but a worthless piece of shit! Cappi thought to himself about Cesare.

When he saw Cesare and Rah pull off, he was pissed. It was bad enough that he didn't show up for work, but he still had to pay him at the end of the week for doing absolutely nothing. When he should have been learning all he could from Cappi about the club, Cesare chose to flirt with the strippers and barmaids all night long instead. Geno tasked him with teaching Cesare about how to run the strip club so that when the time was right for Cappi to move up in the organization, Cesare could take over as the new manager. However, being truthful, Cesare wasn't management material at all. There was nothing that Geno could do or say to convince Cappi otherwise. He was forced to endure his presence because Geno was the Boss and what he said was law. He had no choice but to play his position. Cappi reached onto his hip and pulled out his cell phone to call Cesare. Of course, as expected, he didn't answer the phone. He decided to leave him a message.

Cesare, you know who this is, man. You're late once again, but what's new about that, huh? I need you here at the club tonight. I have to take care of some other business tonight and I need you to cover for me. Give me a call when you get this message ASAP! Cappi barked into the phone before he hung up.

Cappi made no mention of the fact he just saw him pull off from in front of the club because it was pointless. Their so called business arrangement made his blood pressure boil, but he bit the bullet and took it like a soldier. He kept his focus on the end game, which was to move on to making more money in another more lucrative area of the Caprese empire.

Cappi, at five feet and three inches tall, was diminutive in stature, but strong as an ox. He went to the gym at least five times a week to lift weights. His massive biceps and triceps were the end result. He could bench press over three hundred pounds easily. He looked like a smaller version of Lou Ferrigno, with the same dark hair and broad nose. Being short gave him a complex, but over time, he learned to use it to his advantage.

Growing up, he used to get picked on a lot because of his size. However, when his father enrolled him in the local Boys & Girls Club, he developed an interest in boxing. Over time, he became one helluva fighter. He went on to win several Golden Gloves championships in his weight class. Once he honed his craft, none of the older and taller dudes in their neighborhood dared to mess with him or else they could expect to take a butt whipping. After he made an example out of a few of them, the message was clear- little Cappi was not the one to mess with anymore.

Cappi and Geno bonded over their love of boxing and being a rebel. As teenagers, the two of them used to run a pickpocket scam on tourists in downtown Baltimore at the Inner Harbor. Every weekend during the summer they would search for the perfect vic amongst the many out of town tourists to rob. They never got caught and got away with a good amount of money which they blew partying and chasing girls. They used to pick fights with the upper class boys in high school because they knew none of them could beat them, either one on one or together, in a fight. They would shake them down for their lunch money as well. Whenever one of them resisted, they didn't hesitate to administer a beat down to further persuade the poor fool to give up his funds.

Cappi almost beat one kid to death when he made a pass at one of his girlfriends. The brutal beating got him expelled from school and landed him in a juvenile detention facility.

Over the years, he served several stints in jail for violent assaults and attempted murder charges. It was only natural that he became one of the Caprese family's top enforcers. He was comfortable committing murder if it served to benefit the cause of the Caprese family. The streets had to get the message clearly that they were not to be taken lightly and any acts of aggression against them would be met with an even more brutal response.

Even though he started out as Geno's best friend, over time, he developed a closer relationship with Silvio. When Geno graduated from high school and decided to go to college, their relationship was never the same. Cappi was a street cat to his core, whereas Geno wanted to be both a legitimate business man and a gangster. Cappi didn't share his vision because he felt that a man couldn't live in both worlds at the same time. At some point, he would have to make a choice between the two. Cappi loved robbing banks and pulling off heists or breaking a few bones because it gave him a rush like nothing else in life. He wanted no parts of a corporate board room like Geno did. If you gave him a burner and a well laid out plan to pull off a bank robbery or a scheme to rob a jewelry store, then he was in his element.

Geno could have that fairy tale white house with a picket fence and the wife and two kids version of the American dream life. It wasn't for him.

Silvio shared Cappi's same mindstate and that was why they became so tight. They did all of the dirty work for the Caprese crew while Geno was the legitimate face of the family that the world saw. People feared Geno not because of anything that he did himself, but because of all of the countless bodies that Cappi and Silvio caught in the process of carving out territory for the crew. It was their high propensity for violence that made the family a force to be reckoned with in the criminal underworld. They brought in the dirty money while Geno and his team of bankers and business associates cleaned it up and turned it into significant profits from legitimate businesses that they all enjoyed the spoils of for many years. However, Silvio and Cappi didn't feel as though they got the recognition for their efforts that they deserved from Geno. They felt as though after Geno obtained his college degrees, he saw himself as being better than them. They believed that he acted like they were his workers, as opposed to his business partners. If they had their way, that was about to change very soon.

Cappi was a risk taker and never played it safe. His name meant "lucky" in Italian and it fit him just right. His good luck always seemed to work whenever he went to the casinos. He loved to gamble and he usually won big at the blackjack tables.   Geno used to call him his good luck charm whenever he used to accompany him to Atlantic City or Las Vegas to gamble because he won big when they were together.   In addition to gambling, he loved fast cars and pretty women.   Those were his two vices.   He drove around town in his supercharged Ford Mustang or his money green Chevrolet Camaro.   He didn't care for the far more flashy European sports cars like the Lamborghini or Porsche.   He was a fanatic for the classic American muscle cars.   He loved to air them out on the highway to enjoy the rush of going as fast as he could.

Cappi also loved to chase the ladies just as much as he loved his cars.   He could never turn down a pretty face attached to a slim waist and nicely shaped butt.   That was why Geno had him in charge of the strip club and the illegal whorehouses that they ran across the city.   He had a way with the ladies and knew how to handle them just right to keep them motivated to bring in good money for the organization.   He was a firm, but fair pimp.   He knew when to show affection to his female workers and when to administer discipline.

Cappi stood out in front of Lila's and inhaled the toxic smoke from his cancer stick.   He was a chain smoker for as long as he could remember with a two pack of cigarettes a day habit.   He let out a loud hacking cough and spit out brown resin filled phlegm onto the ground after he inhaled the toxic fumes into his lungs. His doctor warned him that if he continued to smoke at the rate he did now, he stood a good chance of developing lung cancer. He saw how the disease got the best of Leonardo, but he didn't care. When he finished his cigarette, he threw the butt on to the ground and walked back into the club.

The loud music blared from the speakers while the girls danced on the center stage. He walked over to the bar area where Silvio was seated. He had a drink in one hand and his other one wrapped around the waist of one of the club's newest dancers, Sparkle. He enjoyed her company. As one of the heads of the Caprese family, being able to sample some of the finest young tender kittens for free was one of the many perks he took advantage of on a regular basis. His mind was filled with images of what he planned to do with Sparkle tonight when her shift was over. He whispered something sweet in her ear to make her smile. He was so caught up in his conversation he didn't hear Cappi walk up behind him and tap him on the shoulder. He instantly jump out of his seat and got into a defensive position, ready to fight. When he saw it was Cappi, he relaxed.

"You can't be sneaking up on me like that, Cappi. I almost laid you out with this lethal left hand of mine," Silvio uttered.

"The only time that left hand is lethal is when you're jerking off, you big lug," Cappi joked. Silvio laughed as well. He playfully grabbed Cappi up into a headlock. He didn't take offense to Cappi's jab at him because they cut up like this on a regular basis. When he let him go, Cappi threw a quick punch to Silvio's midsection that bounced off of his solid stomach muscles.

"Can you excuse us for a minute, Sparkle? We have to discuss some business. Daddy will get back with you in a few."

"Of course, I can. You two boys don't hurt each other now," Sparkle said playfully in her most innocent voice. She wore her long blonde hair in two ponytails. She was dressed in a school uniform because it was a part of her stage routine. Both Cappi and Silvio's eyes were locked in on her firm backside when she walked away from them and headed toward the stage. She was the next girl scheduled to dance for their eagerly awaiting customers.

"That is one fine piece of ass right there. I could fit my whole hand in that gap between her thighs," Cappi imagined. He was into rough, kinky sex and fantasized about what he wanted to do to her.

"Be easy, Cappi. I've got that one covered. The only thing that's going up in that sweet little trap is me and Mr. Johnson here," Silvio joked but he was dead serious. He and Cappi normally had their way with most of the girls at the club, but Sparkle was different. Silvio genuinely had a thing for her and had no intention of sharing her with Cappi.

"She's all yours, Sil. Enough about that chick, let's talk about business. You know that little prick of a brother of yours was just outside with that Rastafarian friend of his. I just missed him before he pulled off. He was supposed to work tonight, but this is the third time he was a no show this week. All he wants to do is smoke weed and chase women. This little arrangement we have is not working out, Sil," Cappi advised him.

"Yeah, I know my little brother is a mess right now, but what are we gonna do? Geno busts his balls enough as it is. The kid's trying to find himself. Give him some time. He'll be alright," Silvio replied.

"I hear you, Sil. The kid needs to get himself together soon. I don't need the deadweight around me. I mean I am running a business here, you know? On another note, are you ready for this meeting that we have coming up?" Cappi asked him. He ordered a glass of Crown Royal with no ice from the bartender. He knew Silvio felt uncomfortable talking about Cesare, but he didn't care. Cappi always kept it real and spoke honestly from the heart.

"I was born ready for this. It's time for me to get back what was stolen from me. Are you having second thoughts?" Silvio asked in return.

"Not at all, I just want you to be sure about this move because once it's set in motion, there's no turning back," Cappi stated firmly while he sipped his drink.

Silvio's issues with Geno were deeply rooted. As the oldest and the most eager to find favor with their father, he was the first one of the Caprese boys to get into trouble with the law. He had no interest whatsoever in living a legitimate lifestyle. All he ever wanted to be was a thug. All throughout grade school he was suspended repeatedly for getting into fights and for being disruptive in class.

Silvio dropped out of high school and assembled a small group of his friends from the neighborhood and began to steal expensive European cars. They sold the stolen cars to a local chop shop owner, Giovanni Lombardi, who would, in turn, strip the cars down and sell the individual parts for a substantial profit. As time went on, Silvio and his boys saved up enough money to open up their own chop shop and became competition for Giovanni. A battle for control ensued between the two crews and Silvio and his boys wound up killing Giovanni. After his death, the competition ceased.

At just nineteen years old, Silvio proved to be a damn good earner out in the streets. Over time, Silvio expanded his illegal empire to include several whorehouses scattered across the city that brought in major income. He and Geno's little marijuana operation also was in full swing.

However, no matter what Silvio did to prove he was a gangster, he could never find favor with his father. Geno was his favorite son and the one who made him most proud. He grew to not only resent Geno, but his father as well. He feared Leonardo when he was younger, but as age set in, that fear disappeared. Over time, they became more and more distant due to Silvio feeling slighted. He only saw his father during holiday family gatherings because his mother begged him to come. Other than that, he could do without being in his presence.

While Geno followed in Silvio's footsteps and got involved in various illegal acts with him while he was in high school, he also managed to stay in school and get good grades at the same time. Unlike Silvio, he understood the lessons Leonardo tried to impart unto his sons. He tried to teach them that with all of the advancements in technology the Feds and local police had at their disposal to use in their investigations of criminal activity, a gangster couldn't continue to do business the way Silvio planned to run his organization because he viewed it as a suicide mission. If they limited the scope of their business to just earn money illegally, with no legal way to justify at least some of the funds, then it was only a matter of time before the alphabet boys came for them with an indictment on a host of charges.

Leonardo figured it was wiser for his sons to assimilate into the American society as legitimate hard working citizens so their illegal activities weren't as noticeable. That was how old school gangsters rose to power in the seventies and were able to have so much influence in corporate America. Geno was the smartest out of his brothers and got this message loud and clear. It was his primary motivation behind becoming a lawyer. He reasoned that once he knew the ins and outs of the legal system and how to maneuver around it, the Caprese crew would be untouchable by law enforcement. He had the vision and insight that Silvio lacked. He was the brains while Silvio was the brawn of the organization.

Over time, a battle ensued between Geno and Silvio over control of their organization. Silvio was a hothead with a quick temper who made decisions based upon his feelings at the moment whereas Geno was a methodical, level headed thinker who planned out his actions carefully. Silvio was always ready to respond violently to rival crews when they tried to move in on their action, while Geno sought to negotiate peaceful ways to develop workable business relationships everybody benefitted from with minimal bloodshed involved. It was Silvio's short temper that led to several of their crew members being killed over the years in unnecessary turf wars. His temper also led to him being arrested on an assault charge after he got into a barroom brawl with a complete stranger over a woman. Silvio wound up serving three years in jail for the assault charge.

While he was incarcerated, Geno seized the opportunity to take over as the leader of the family and to run things his way. He had sit down meetings with rival bosses Silvio had beef with and worked out mutually beneficially business arrangements that put an end to the bloodshed between them. He took the family's dirty money and laundered it, with the help of some of his former college classmates who worked in the banking industry and who were open to making a little extra money on the side. He was able to set up legitimate businesses that would generate revenue that the federal government couldn't touch if they ever came after the family. Under Silvio's leadership, the Caprese family was known as a force to be reckoned with out in the streets. With Geno in charge, they became a force in the business world as well. This marked the beginnings stages of the development of the Caprese Foundation.

The changes Geno implemented while Silvio was gone initially caused some friction with the lower level foot soldiers. Even though he was gone, many of them were still loyal to Silvio for whatever reason. However, after they saw an increase in pay under Geno, their uneasiness with Geno's leadership subsided. Geno was a businessman first and foremost. He knew the value in making sure that he kept them all well fed. They made far more money under Geno's leadership than they did under Silvio, who would only break them off a small percentage of whatever job they pulled off. The acceptance of the organizational structure that Geno put in place was evident when Silvio was released from prison. When he tried to resume control of the family at that time, Geno wasn't willing to give up his leadership role as they previously agreed that he would. Geno now felt he was better suited for the job.

Unable to reach a compromise to share control of the family, it was put to a vote. The crew voted almost unanimously to keep Geno as its leader, with Silvio as his second in command. Silvio, not wanting to engage in an all out war with his brother, accepted the demotion gracefully, but he never got over his little brother's power play. He felt that he was cheated out of a position that he deserved and would not rest until he got it back.

"I'm good with the situation exactly how we discussed that it will play out. We've been earning out in the streets for a lot of years and now it's time for us to really eat. Geno shouldn't be the only one living like a king out here. It's our time. This is a dangerous task to take on, but I'm willing to gamble that we'll come out on top. We just have to make sure that there are no mistakes. The risk is worth the reward," Silvio stated resolutely.

"You don't have to say anymore then, partner. It's a done deal," Cappi stated just as confidently.

They both ordered a shot of tequila and toasted to their grand plan being a successful one. They followed up those shots with several more. If everything went how they hoped it would, life was about to change for both of them very quickly.

Chapter 11

Silvio and Cappi chose a secluded section of Druid Hill Park as the location of the big meeting that they scheduled. The area was dark and somewhere people rarely ventured off to when they were in the park. They were the first ones to arrive. Cappi, in the driver's seat, parked the car, turned off the engine, and dimmed the headlights. He pulled out a cigarette from his pack and lit it up. He placed it up to his lips and sucked up the tobacco into his lungs to calm his uneasy nerves down. Silvio shot a disgusted look over in his direction.

"What the hell are you looking at me like that for, Sil?" he asked.

"Roll the Goddamn window down you asshole. I don't want to smell that shit," Silvio replied. He was a non-smoker and hated the smell of cigarettes. The scent gave him a headache and made his nose run. Plus, he didn't want to damage his healthy lungs with secondhand smoke.

"Hey, I'm sorry about that, Sil. I forget sometimes," Cappi attempted to apologize. He hit the button on the door of his Lincoln MKZ to roll down the window so the smoke fumes could escape out of the car and blend in with the night air.

The two engaged in small talk about the recent NBA playoffs and a host of other business related matters they needed to handle. Their conversation was interrupted when they saw a black limousine pull up in front of them. The bright headlights aimed in their direction temporarily blinded them. Before they got out of the car, they made sure their guns were locked and loaded and ready to fire just in case things went off course and they had to shoot their way out of this situation. This was a high risk meeting and anything could happen. He and Silvio got out of their car and walked over toward the vehicle. As they approached the limo, the rear door opened up and out stepped the man they had waited for, Liddell Coker.

Liddell stood six feet and six inches tall. He had long tree trunk arms that were packed with muscles. He was surrounded by four dreadlock wearing goons armed with semiautomatic weapons. None of his men looked afraid to use them. Tight security was paramount for him in his line of work. He made a lot of enemies because of the unscrupulous way he conducted business. His word was never his bond and he always had a sneaky look on his face that suggested he was not an individual to be trusted. Back in Jamaica, he was well known for committing many brutal murders with his bare hands. He was dressed in a black suit like he just came from a funeral.

"Ahh, gentleman, I'm glad you decided to show up. I hope you have had some time to consider my proposal," Ledell spoke in his deep baritone voice.

"Your offer was very generous. However, how do we know that you can deliver to us what you promised?" Silvio asked him directly.

"My friends, just as sure as the sky is blue and the Earth is round, when Liddell Coker says that he can make something happen, he makes it happen. Me give you my word and make it my bond," he replied calmly. He almost sounded sincere, but with individuals like Liddell, there always was a covert agenda they kept hidden until the proper moment was present for it to surface. He lived for the sneak attack because he maneuvered in such a slimy way, his enemies never saw him coming.

"And what about the backlash that might come as a result of this if we go along with your plan? This is a risky situation. We don't want to be left with our balls hanging out there," Silvio reasoned.

"You don't have to worry about a thing. I have all of the bases covered. You just do your part and I will make you both very rich men. However, if you come up short, there is nowhere you'll be able to hide on this Earth that I won't find you," Liddell replied. His words weren't a threat. They were a promise that he planned to deliver on.

Recently, Liddell had decided that he no longer wanted to be in business with his cousin, Nesta. It wasn't because of any friction between them or because they didn't make a lot of money together. They got along well and the money flowed freely in both of their directions. However, Liddell's greedy nature made it inevitable that he wouldn't be able to share the wealth with another boss for but so long before he wanted it all to himself.

Liddell came up with a plan to take over the joint drug operation which he shared control of with Nesta to make himself the sole boss of the entire organization. He knew Nesta would never go for this new arrangement and planned to have him killed to bring his plan into fruition. He wanted Silvio and Cappi to do the hit so it wouldn't look like an inside job. Nesta was his first cousin, but he didn't care. He stood in the way of him expanding his wealth and power and had to be removed as an obstacle. Liddell was the personification of pure evil.

Liddell's grand scheme didn't end there. He also had his eyes set on taking over all of the

Jackson brothers' drug corners in East Baltimore. That wouldn't happen without a bloody battle because Milton and Jarvis wouldn't go out without a fight. Liddell already had soldiers in place to go to war with them, but he needed valuable Intel on the ins and outs of their operation to give him the needed advantage to attack them most efficiently and effectively. That was where Silvio came into play. He knew the structure of their organization from all angles because he dealt with them on a daily basis. In exchange for his help, Liddell promised Silvio that they would become equal partners in the East Baltimore territory. That would mean a major bump in pay for Silvio from what he currently received as Geno's top underboss. The same held true for Cappi, who he planned to make his second in charge. They were thirsty for a come up.

Silvio knew he would have to kill Geno as well if he wanted to make this plan work. Even though he was his own brother, it didn't matter. He was tired of playing second fiddle to him and wanted his seat at the head of the throne that he felt Geno stole from him while he was in jail. Envy was like a cancer that ate away at his heart and didn't allow for him to feel love for Geno like he should for his own brother. He couldn't stand Geno's elitist attitude. Plus, he was tired of doing all of the dirty work for the Caprese family just for Geno to get all of the credit for their wealth and power. He wanted his chance to shine again. This was his shot to make that happen.

"Well, then we have a deal," Silvio shot back at him. He was never the type of man to be moved by a threat because Silvio was just as deadly as Liddell. They were cut from the same cloth. He, too, planned to have a contingency plan in place just in case their plan backfired on them.

"It will be a pleasure doing business with you. I will be in touch soon so that we can set this plan in motion. You gentleman enjoy your evening," Liddell stated. He shook hands with both Silvio and Cappi to solidify their agreement before he walked back over to his limousine and pulled off.

"This is it, Sil. There's no turning back now," Cappi stated half heartedly. He was partially torn between the brotherhood that he once shared with Geno and the desire he had for more money and power. He knew he would never get what he felt was his just due from Geno so he had to take it, by any means necessary. This was his shot and he didn't want to let it pass him by.

"I'm ready," Silvio stated without a hint of trepidation in his voice. His mind was made up. They had just upped the stakes in the game. It would be a winner take all type of situation and they didn't plan to lose.

Chapter 12

Geno had just finished up another successful morning in court when he decided to stop by Maggie's to grab a bite to eat before he headed back to the office to take care of a few things. Along the way, he called Sal and told him to meet him there so they could talk. Sal was his sounding board for new business ideas and he trusted his opinion. Unlike Silvio and Cappi, Sal shared his vision and understood the need for them all to work toward legitimizing their business operation on an entirely different level. Geno couldn't discuss company branding or his marketing strategies with Silvio and Cappi like he could with Sal because those kinds of things didn't hold their interest. If the conversation wasn't about taking down another big score or moving a shipment of drugs, they could care less. All they cared about was the end result. However Geno went about doubling or tripling their money was his business. They just wanted to enjoy the spoils of being rich, but didn't want to put in the kind of hard work in the office like Geno did.

Sal shared the same mindset that Geno had because even though he was every bit of a ruthless thug as Silvio and Cappi when it was necessary, he also had a keen business mind. He took a few college courses in Marketing and Economics when he was in his twenties, but he never stuck around to get his college degree. Instead, he studied every book he could on his own on the subjects to expand his knowledge base. He was well versed enough to be able to hold an intelligent conversation with any Ivy League educated corporate executive. He helped Geno develop the marketing plan they used to make the Caprese Foundation saleable to their legitimate business partners when they convinced them to invest their money into the joint business ventures they proposed. He was good at what he did and that was why Geno made him his right hand man in their legitimate business dealings.

"So, what's this big idea that you have brewing, Geno? I know you and you've been secretive about this one so it has to be big," Sal prodded him for more information. They both feasted on a big plate of lasagna and washed it down with a bottle of wine while they talked.

"You know me well, Sal. This idea that I'm working on is going to change the game for us and put us in a different category of success than any other gangsters before us. I'm taking this thing to another level," Geno bragged.

"Well, let me hear this genius idea then, Geno. Come on and spit out," Sal egged him on further.

To satisfy his good friend's curiosity, Geno elaborated on his grand scheme that he had. He broke down the ins and outs of his plan to Sal, who listened attentively to every word. He asked him questions to clarify what he didn't understand and Geno came right back at him with thorough responses. When Geno was done, he awaited Sal's feedback.

"So, is this pure genius or what? Do you think we can pull it off?"

"Geno, you never cease to amaze me. I don't how these ideas pop into that brain of yours. If you can pull this off, my respect for you will go to another level," Sal replied.

"That's what I like to hear. We can leave the petty street money alone and be the kind of Bosses that the world will respect. We can take a seat next to Warren Buffett and Bill Gates. They will have no choice but to give us our props. Our money will be long enough that it can do all of the talking for us."

"I absolutely agree. My only concern is if we can get everybody on the board to play ball with us and make this happen. All we need is for them to disapprove of this move and it's a wrap," Sal cautioned him.

All of the foundation's board members had a vote on all final decisions made. However, Geno was the majority shareholder so his voice carried the most weight. Milton and Jarvis were also members of the board and he knew that he could count on their votes as well. As for the rest of his board members, Geno was sure that he could persuade them to go along with him in making this venture happen. If they didn't vote in his favor willingly, he had enough dirt on them to blackmail them to force their hand to go along with him.

"I'm not really worried about that all. If they can't see the brilliance of this idea, then I have a backup plan in place to ensure that they will not be an obstacle. This is going to happen. The big prize we've been looking for is now within our reach, Sal, and I'm not letting it get away," Geno advised him.

"Well, you know where my loyalty stands. That is never to be questioned. I ride with you until the end," Sal stated resolutely.

"Loyalty over everything, that's what I like to hear. Let's toast to success," Geno suggested as he raised his glass.

"To success," Sal stated while he raised his glass as well. They both took man sized gulps of wine to the head in a manner only appropriate for two bosses to do.

For the next hour or so, they sat back and talked about a host of other topics while they finished their meal. It was refreshing for Geno to not have to talk about street business all of the time like he did with Silvio. As time ticked away, Geno looked at his watch and realized he needed to get back to the office. Just as he was about to stand up to leave, Geno noticed a familiar face enter the restaurant. It was Nesta, flanked by two of his henchmen, and he was headed in their direction. He was surprised to see him because he never came to Maggie's before. Also, he thought he made it clear to him when they first started doing business that they shouldn't be seen in public together. Geno's relaxed mood now turned into a tense one.

Nesta Clarke had a meek physical appearance. He stood close to six feet tall and was rail thin. In his early forties, he had streaks of grey throughout his long dreadlocks that hung down his lower back. He wore horn rimmed glasses that made him look more like a nerdy scientist than a crime boss. He was dressed in a pair of jeans and a t-shirt emblazoned with the logo of the Jamaican national soccer team. He didn't fancy expensive three piece suits like Geno, but his attire didn't make him any less of a businessman. His mind was equally as sharp as Geno's was and his Jamaican posse was just as deadly as Geno's crew.

"Nesta, what brings you down to this neck of the woods? This is far away from your West Baltimore turf, wouldn't you say?" Geno quizzed him.

"Be easy, Geno, I come in peace. I've been trying to get a hold of you, but you have not returned any of my calls. Should I be concerned about our relationship?" Nesta asked as he helped himself to a seat at their table. His men positioned themselves behind him.

Nesta had called Geno several times in the past few weeks, but Geno never returned his calls because he knew exactly what he wanted. It was the same old plea he had heard numerous times before. Nesta wanted to become a partner in the Caprese Foundation. Geno had no intention of making him a business partner in the foundation, no matter how many times he asked. He liked Nesta and respected his business acumen, but he simply did not trust him to a degree that he felt comfortable enough to let him in on the inner workings of his organization. He saw too much of himself in Nesta. Men like them always had grand aspirations of achieving more power and wealth and would do so by unscrupulous means. He didn't need another person around him that he would have to constantly watch his back around because he feared him coming for his top spot.

Geno also thought he made it clear to Nesta they didn't do business with one another directly, but that all interaction with him was to go through Silvio. To see him front and center at his place of business caused him great concern. He wanted no connection to ever be drawn between the two of them because it could possibly do damage to the public persona that he worked so hard to create. He wondered how Nesta even knew he was there at the moment. He surmised that somebody had to let him know, but he had no clue who it was. He wondered if he was being watched. Nesta's presence made him feel uneasy. Geno was glad he had his pistol inside of the holster underneath his suit jacket just in case it was necessary for him to draw down on Nesta and his crew. He knew that Sal packed his heat as well. Several of his soldiers were on point throughout the restaurant ready to spring into action if necessary.

"I'm not sure what you mean by that exactly. Do you care to elaborate?"

"I certainly can elaborate. I'm not going to waste your time so I'll get right to the point. It has been brought to my attention by a mutual business associate of ours that you are putting together a massive business deal that could bring in billions of dollars and I want in on it," Nesta stated rather directly.

Geno was caught totally off guard. Even though he and Nesta traveled in similar business circles and had relationships with some of the same wealthy philanthropists, he was careful that he took his proposal to investors that he was sure he could trust to be discreet. He wondered which one of his potential investors for his newest business venture leaked information to Nesta. His plan was supposed to be kept under wraps until he revealed it at the right time. He had to find the source of the leak to do damage control. He did his best to not show his hand to Nesta to give off the vibe he was uncomfortable with the conversation.

"You must have been given some bad information, Nesta. I have no clue what you're talking about," Geno shot back at him. He could sense Nesta knew he had just lied, but he didn't care. He still put on his best poker face.

"Don't insult me, Geno. Are you trying to tell me that my money is good with you in the streets, but not in the legitimate business world as well? I hope that is not what you are trying to tell me. I would hate to feel that way," Nesta threatened him indirectly.

"Your feelings are your feelings, Nesta. I have nothing to do with that at all. As I stated, I have no clue what you are talking about. You should tell whoever gave you that information that passing off bad information about my alleged business dealings is libelous and subject to a stiff penalty," Geno countered with a veiled threat of his own.

"I hear you, Geno. I hear you loud and clear," Nesta stated with a hint of disappointment in his voice.

"Now if you don't mind, I would like to get back to my conversation with my good friend Sal here. You should never disturb a man when he is eating. That's rude and borderline disrespectful. I'm trying not to get upset. I think it's best that you leave now before things get out of hand," Geno advised him. He glanced around the restaurant to make sure that his soldiers were on point and ready to spring into action if necessary.

"Have it your way, Geno. We will chat again. Enjoy your meal, my friend."

Nesta got up from the table. He shot a sly grin in Geno's direction while he walked toward the front door. His men followed closely behind him. They exchanged stare downs with Geno's men who were positioned throughout the restaurant. Sal, who sat by quietly, but attentively, during the entire verbal exchange, mustered up the nerve to speak.

"What the hell was that about?" Sal asked.

"We need to set up a meeting. Get Silvio and Cappi and the rest of the crew together. We may have a problem on our hands," Geno replied honestly.

He yearned for the day he could leave behind the need to resort to his lower self to maintain peace and order in his line of business, but sometimes there was no other way. Geno knew Nesta was a man much like himself in terms of character and demeanor. Neither one of them handled rejection well. If Nesta was bold enough to come to his place of business to plead his case to be included in on his business deal, then he wouldn't rest until he got what he wanted. Geno had no intention of changing his mind so he knew he had to brace himself for some form of offensive move from Nesta to try and force his hand. However Nesta chose to come at him, he would be prepared.

Chapter 13

Nesta sat in the back of his limousine with a chicanerous grin on his face. He loved it when he could make a man tremble just by his mere presence. That was how he perceived Geno felt when he saw him walk into his restaurant boldly and approach him so aggressively. However, the anger he just displayed toward Geno for not cutting him in on his big business deal was just a facade to get just the reaction he got from him. He sipped on a Red Parrot beer and crossed his legs. He offered a beer to his two traveling companions, but they declined.

"Your plan worked like a charm. Geno looked like he saw the devil himself when I walked into that place, Mon. Him was scared to death. I swear he must have pissed in him pants. That boy don't want no trouble with me," Nesta uttered to Silvio and Cappi.

"I know my brother. He's a smart business man, but he ain't got the heart for the nuts and bolts of this street shit. I'm the reason that he's so feared out here. I'm the killer in the family," Silvio bragged proudly.

"Yeah, we're the ones that put in all of the work that keeps the money coming in for the family while he cleans it up and breaks us off a small piece of the pie. We take all of the risks out here on the front line, but he keeps the lion's share of the wealth to himself. What kind of shit is that?" Cappi asked.

"I hear you, Mon. I hear you. This guy Geno has what Me call a God complex. Him thinks that the Sun rises and sets with him. He thinks him shit don't stink like the rest of ours do. Me can't wait to see his face when him come tumbling down that mountain top that he set himself up on," Nesta joked.

"It's about time somebody gave him a reality check. If he wasn't my brother, I would have iced him years ago," Silvio confessed.

He never got over the fact that Geno cleverly unseated him as the head of the family business that he started or that he was able to convince all of the soldiers in their squad to go along with him. However, Geno knew how to make them more money than Silvio did and that was a fact. In the streets, he who held the bigger pot of gold had a tendency to carry the most weight and influence amongst a pack of hungry wolves.

To take a back seat to his little brother was insult that he simply couldn't accept. It made him feel incompetent. Now he had a chance to get revenge and to flip the script in his favor.

When Nesta found out from a mutual business associate that Geno was putting out feelers for potential investors for a billion dollar deal, he was impressed by his maneuver and wanted in on the venture himself. Consequently, since he dealt directly with Silvio and had a good rapport with him, he decided to reach out to him first to broker a meeting with Geno.

When he set up a meeting with Silvio to discuss the matter, he was surprised to find out that Silvio had no clue what Geno was up to at all. Silvio felt pissed his brother had something so big planned and he wasn't even included in the conversation. Instead, he chose to involve all of his college educated, white collar criminal cronies in on the deal. His jealousy and rage spilled out in every venomous word he spoke about Geno to Nesta. He couldn't control himself.

Nesta saw this dissension in the ranks as an opportunity to make inroads into their organization. A house divided meant there was a weakness present that he could exploit to his advantage. He tried his hand by dangling a carrot out to Silvio to see if he would bite. Silvio went for the bait without a second thought. He was even more amped up when he found out

Cappi, another one of Geno's top dogs, was also down to do him in.

Nesta proposed to Silvio that he wanted to help him take over the Caprese drug business from the Jackson brothers. In exchange for his help in making that happen, Nesta would make Silvio and Cappi his business partners. He told them they would split all profits in the Jackson brothers' territory equally three ways. This would represent a far larger piece of the action than they received currently under Geno's regime. Personal greed always fed the hunger of a man like Silvio, who had no boundaries on what level he would stoop to in order to obtain power and prestige. He also wanted to take over Geno's legitimate business empire out of spite because he knew how much it meant to him.

Little did Nesta know that his cousin, Liddell, went behind his back and made Silvio and Cappi an offer already to have him killed so he could take over Nesta's portion of their drug organization. Silvio and Cappi hatched a plan of their own in return that was more mutually beneficial for them. They came up with a plan that once Nesta was successful in getting Geno out of the way, they would tell Nesta about Liddell's plan to kill him and put them at war with one another. The goal was for them to either kill each other or at the very least, cripple their organization. At that point, they had it in their minds they would swoop in and take over their drug territory as well. Once it was all said and done, Silvio would be seated in his rightful place as the head of the Caprese family with an even larger empire under his control and Geno would be out of the picture. He would make Cappi his right hand man.

"Me not worried about a thing because Me know that there is a season and a time for everything under the sun. This is my season and this is my time to shine. My friends rest easy and stay sharp. We've got a lot of work to do. Your brother is a smart man. He won't go away as easily as you think. Don't underestimate him. We can't afford to make any mistakes, you understand me?"

"I hear you loud and clear. We'll handle our end of the deal. You just make sure you can deliver as promised, Rasta Man," Silvio shot back.

"It's all good, Mon. Me got this," Nesta stated calmly, but with bold conviction.

He dropped them off around the corner from Lila's. Silvio and Cappi got out of the limo and walked toward the club. Geno had called a meeting there tonight and they were already late.

Chapter 14

Sal did as Geno instructed him to do and rounded up their squad for a sit down meeting. He told everybody to be at Lila's at eight o'clock sharp. Geno was a stickler when it came to being punctual when he called a meeting. If anybody came late, they could expect to be cursed out royally at the very least. Financial fines were also handed down as well if that was how he felt at the moment. It was now fifteen minutes to the hour and their foot soldiers began to arrive. He led them down to a large open space area in the basement of the club. Geno called it The War Room because the only time they had a large meeting like this in the past was when they were about to go to war with a rival crew. This was where they met to discuss strategy and plot their next move. Murder was always the main topic on the agenda.

"Geno, what's going on, my brother? Whatever it is, we're riding with you until the end," Jarvis Jackson stated. His brother Milton stood next to him.

"That's right, Geno, if you've got a problem, then we've got a problem," Milton chimed in.

"That's what I like to hear, fellas," Geno said with a happy look on his face. They walked over to the far end of the room and took a seat.

When Jarvis and Milton arrived, Geno was glad to see them. He embraced them both in a brotherly hug. He would need them in a major way if any drama popped off with Nesta and his rowdy bunch of Jamaican killers. While Geno and his boys were certainly a formidable bunch in their own right, the Jackson brothers provided them with much needed muscle because of the sheer number of deadly soldiers they had under their command who were always ready for some gunplay.

Even though Milton and Jarvis were African American and he was Italian, Geno treated them like family. The only color he acknowledged in his crew was green. They'd always had his back and Geno had theirs in return in whatever way he could. They had held him down in several violent confrontations the Caprese family had out in the streets over the years. Silvio didn't like the close bond between them because of his own racial prejudices against Black men, but

Geno didn't give a damn. He was the boss and set the rules.

Geno sat down at the head of the table and Sal was seated on his left side. There was an empty chair next to him on his right side where Silvio normally sat. Cappi's chair beside Sal was empty as well. It was strange for two of his top underbosses to be absent for this very important meeting. This didn't go unnoticed by Geno. He was pissed off, but kept a smile on his face to hide his anger. If they weren't on time, it made Geno look bad to the rest of his crew. It sent the wrong message that when he gave an order, not everyone had to follow his directive. One thing Geno never tolerated was insubordination. That was when the suit and tie Geno took a back seat and the hoodlum in him took over. He would get his respect, one way or another.

"Where the hell are Cappi and Sil?" he leaned over to ask Sal in a low whisper. Sal simply shrugged his shoulders.

"I have no clue, Geno. I called them both and they said they would be here," Sal replied. He picked up his phone to call them both again, but both of their phones just rung.

"This is unacceptable. When I call a meeting, they need to make sure they're here on time. There is no excuse for this shit," Geno stated angrily.

"I agree, Geno, but what can I do, huh?" Sal stated rhetorically.

Geno instructed two of his young foot soldiers who just walked in the room to sit in their seats. If Silvio and Cappi arrived and had a problem with it, they could take it up with him. It was eight o'clock on the nose and the room was packed. Geno didn't plan to hold up the meeting from starting because of them. He had business to handle. He got everybody to settle down and called the meeting to order.

"I know everybody is wondering what's going on and why you're here. Lately, things have been good out in the streets. Everybody's been making a lot of money with little to no friction from the cops or any of our competition out there. That's how things should be if everybody handles their business accordingly. However, every now and then some brave souls decide to poke their chests out and disrupt the smooth flow of things. Those bold souls have big dreams and aspirations to try and claim somebody else's possessions and make them theirs. When that happens, it's only right that we have to stand firm and defend what's ours by any means necessary. It seems that our Caribbean friends have it in their heads they want to try and expand and become a more integral part of this thing of ours, but I can't let that happen. We can't let that happen. We've worked so hard to build this family up to where it is now and I'll be damned if I let somebody come along and take this from us. I don't know what our friends have up their sleeves, but whatever it is, we will be prepared. I need you all to keep your eyes and ears open for anything that looks suspect. We need to watch each other's backs. If they try to move on us, we will respond with equal and even more brutal force to push them back. This is not a game, but serious business. Anybody in here that's not up for a war, I suggest you high tail it out of here and never let your face be seen again. I only want soldiers around me. Are you with me?" Geno asked.

He awaited their response. A resounding "Hell yeah!" was the consensus opinion throughout the room. When he was midway through his speech, he noticed Silvio and Cappi enter the room. They looked up front and saw the two seats usually reserved for them were filled and felt slighted. Geno cut his eyes in their direction briefly, and continued with his speech.

"So, boss, what do you need us to do? I'm ready to go mount up and lay all of those weed smoking, nappy headed maggots down tonight. They all can get it," Angelo stated with sincere conviction. He was a young, fearless warrior that Sal took under his wing recently. He worked as his personal driver and Sal let him get in on a few robbery jobs he set up to let him get his feet wet. He was eager to prove himself worthy of being a made man. To catch a body would be a surefire way to make his case.

"I appreciate your energy, Angelo; however, we need to be smart about how we handle this situation. It's never wise to rush into battle. We must be patient and not tip our hand to our opponent because that gives them an advantage. Before we strike, we observe their every move and action to see when the time is right. I need you all to be sharp out in those streets and have each other's backs. Nobody is to make a move unless they get an order from me or Sal. If and when it's time to make a move, we'll hit'em hard and make it swift with no errors," Geno stated explicitly.

He sounded like an Army general instead of a crime boss. His speech resembled a lesson out of Sun Tzu's book, Art *of War.* When Silvio heard him refer to Sal as his right hand, he was heated. That was his position. It only added to the emotional disconnect that existed between him and Geno. After he said a few more words to his troops, Geno ended the meeting. His soldiers slowly exited the room to go about their separate ways for the rest of the night. When the room was empty, he wasted no time tearing into Cappi and Silvio.

"Where the fuck were you two at?" Geno barked.

"I apologize Geno," Cappi stated humbly, but with no explanation.

"Hey, hold up, lil bro, the aggression is not necessary. Let's talk to each other like men here. We got caught up in the middle of taking care of another situation and ran a little late is all," Silvio attempted to explain.

"I'll decide what's necessary because the last time I checked, I ran this crew and not you, Silvio. How do you think it makes me look when I call a meeting and two of my top guys are not here? It makes me look like I'm not in control. You better not let it happen again," Geno threatened.

"Have it your way, Boss. You're the man. I don't want any problems," Silvio stated sarcastically. Truth be told, the way Geno just talked to him only solidified in his mind what he had already set in motion was the right move to make.

"Sal, fill them in on what's going on. I gotta get out of here," Geno stated. He was clearly irritated.

Geno made his way toward the door to exit the room. He was flanked by several of his soldiers who would serve as security for him just in case Nesta decided to make a move. He walked upstairs to make his way to the front door. Along the way, he made a phone call. He was stressed and needed to get home to his family. The sight of them would ease his mind momentarily.

Chapter 15

Leonardo Caprese was situated in his favorite lounge chair in his living room with the remote control in his hand. He flipped through the channels until he came across a station that showed old rerun episodes of his favorite show, *Baretta*. Even though he had watched every episode of the show multiple times, he never got tired of seeing them again and again. He had the dialogue committed to memory and would do his rendition of his favorite scenes right along with the actors. The star of the show, Robert Blake, was one of his favorite actors, along with Robert Deniro and Al Pacino. When he wasn't watching *Baretta*, he would get Marietta to pop in a DVD copy of gangster movies like *The Godfather, Goodfellas, Casino, and A Bronx Tale*. He loved to see actors of Italian descent emulate the gangster lifestyle that he really lived in his heyday. They reminded him of the best years of his life when he was in the thick of all of the action.

Lately, Leonardo didn't have much of a reason to smile. With his health failing, he had more bad days than good. His body ached so bad at times that it was hard for him to get out of bed for days on end. He was in so much pain because the cancer cells that started out in his lungs had spread to his bones. He was burdened by a hacking cough that sometimes forced him to cough up blood. He experienced frequent episodes of shortness of breath and had to wear an oxygen mask. Since being diagnosed, he did one round of chemotherapy, but it failed to improve his health. He tried herbal remedies that were just as ineffective. Leonardo accepted that he had far less days ahead of him than he did behind him. His doctors gave him another six months to live, but he was determined to prove them wrong. He lived his life on his own terms and for him to go out any other way would go against the very nature of his being.

With all of the men he killed and the attempts that were made on his life, Leonardo had cheated death more times than any man should be allowed to do so. He knew he would have to atone for his sins one day and was okay with that reality. Most of his life, he stayed in tip top physical shape and for his body to ravaged by such a debilitating disease was life's most brutal form of karma.

In his best years, he made more money than he knew what to do with and enjoyed every penny. He had traveled all around the world and experienced the best of different cultures. He had his fair share of sexual experiences with herds of beautiful women that would make a porn star want to sit back and take notes. He owned all of the fancy cars and jewelry that his money could buy. He raised his sons to the best of his ability and made sure his sweet Marietta would be taken care of whenever death called his name. For a person that society labeled a public menace and criminal, he felt he had done enough good to make it into Heaven when he transitioned over to the other side. He truly lived a full life and had no room to complain about a thing.

"Hey, Marietta, bring me a little taste of something," he barked. Even though he was terminally sick, it didn't stop him from drinking alcohol. He figured it wouldn't do any more damage to his body than what cancer had already done.

"You know you don't make any sense at all sitting here with an oxygen mask on drinking liquor as if you're not sick enough already," Marietta scolded him while she made his favorite drink, a Manhattan cocktail. The drink was a mixture of rye whiskey, sweet vermouth, and bitters. It was topped off with a cherry. Even though it tasted sweet, it packed a mean punch. The Manhattan was the drink of choice for gangsters in his day. Leonardo was old school in every sense of the word.

"Quit it with the yapping and just do what I asked you, woman."

"Here you go, you old fart," Marietta replied while she handed him his drink. Leonardo took a sip and smiled. The taste of the drink pleased his taste buds.

"Thanks, doll. You're a sweetheart," Leonardo said in a softer tone. He smacked her on her rear end when she walked back into the kitchen. Even though he was sick, he hadn't lost the playful spirit that attracted her to him when they first met. She was still his favorite girl in the world.

Marietta was the epitome of a mobster's wife. She had the tough, spunky attitude to match wits with a hardcore tough guy like Leonardo, but was still a lady in the purest sense of the word. She knew when to be submissive to her man and when to stand up for herself and what she believed to be right. She was okay with being a stay at home mother and raising his three sons while Leonardo earned out in the streets. Whenever he got arrested and had to serve jail time, she had no problem stepping up to the plate and taking care of the family on her own. She was loyal to a fault to Leonardo even though she knew he had other women. She reasoned that it came with the lifestyle and didn't complain as long as she remained number one.

Leonardo loved all of his sons, but Geno was clearly his favorite son out of the three. They all reminded him of himself in different stages in his life. His youngest, Cesare, made him think of how he used to be when he was a young teenage punk in his old Brooklyn neighborhood in search of his self-identity. Just like Cesare got into trouble all of the time for petty things, he was the same way at his age until a few older gangsters took him under their wing. As for Silvio, he got his quick temper and violent nature honestly. He reminded him of himself when he was in his prime and made the bulk of his money taking contract hits. Leonardo was brutal and took pride in his work just like Silvio enjoyed inflicting pain on his victims.

Over the years, he learned to use his brains more than his brawn because he wanted to move up in the ranks of his crime family. When he did this, he went from being a foot soldier in the thick of things to fulfilling a leadership role as an underboss. That was why he was sent to Baltimore to carve out a territory he could control for the family. He had put in enough work in the streets to earn his position and to reap the monetary benefits which came along with the distinguished title. When he looked at Geno today and how he ran the Caprese Foundation, he saw him as the ultimate fulfillment of the life of a made man. Geno was able to maintain his street credibility while he infiltrated corporate America. He had the best of both worlds. The bosses from the old school would be proud of his accomplishments.

Even though he viewed himself as a good father, he knew he was not without faults. He had secrets from his past he knew would come back to haunt him and his family. One secret, in particular, ate at him more than the rest. He had kept it to himself because he knew that if he revealed it to his sons, they would never forgive him or understand his decision to keep it a secret. Given that he was near death, he didn't want to go to his grave without getting it off of his chest.

Leonardo sipped on his drink and glanced at a picture of the only woman that he ever loved anywhere near as much as he did Marietta. A tear formed in the corner of his eye when he thought about her and how much he missed her since she died over ten years ago. He tried to figure out the right words to say to Geno when he saw him later on in the week. He chose to tell him his secret first because he was the most level headed of his sons. He hoped that he would hear him out completely and try to understand things from his point of view. He wasn't sure of the outcome of this conversation, but he had to take that chance. It was the only way he could relieve himself of such a great mental and emotional burden.

Chapter 16

The central office for the Caprese Foundation was located in downtown Baltimore inside of the TransAmerica tower on Light Street. The forty story skyscraper was the largest building in the entire state of Maryland and one of the largest such structures on the East Coast. It was once the home to large corporations like the insurance powerhouse, USF&G, and asset manager corporation, Legg Mason, Inc. Several prominent law firms in the Baltimore area also made the building their home. It was no accident that Geno chose the TransAmerica tower to be the central location for his business empire. It was his way of announcing to the world that the Caprese Foundation was a force to be reckoned with in corporate America alongside all of the prior and present business entities that chose to house their companies within the building.

Geno demanded his seat at the table and to be recognized as a shrewd businessman and not just a defense attorney who was perceived as someone who always fought for the bad guys. He wanted everybody to know that the Italian street kid from Little Italy had arrived and achieved a level of success which rivaled some of the best business minds trained in Ivy League schools. Everybody knew about his father's reputation as a notorious crime figure. The Caprese Foundation was his way of turning the negative perception of his family into a positive one. His legitimate business success fulfilled his father's vision and was a testament to all of his hard work. He was successful in his mission because the Caprese Foundation currently had a net worth of close to two hundred million dollars.

The Caprese Foundation occupied four spacious floors within the building. The law firm was housed on two of the floors. Geno was the senior partner and he had three junior partners, along with several staff attorneys and paralegals that worked alongside him. The third floor was home for the administrative staff that oversaw the daily activities for the many small business ventures the foundation had a financial stake in. Geno had a modest staff of twenty-five employees who worked in this department. The fourth floor was the office for Caprese Innovative Technology Designs, or more commonly known by the acronym (CITD). Next to his law firm, this company was Geno's most prized possession. It brought in the most money by far of all of his business acquisitions in the shortest period of time.

CITD was a video gaming software development firm that he acquired a controlling interest in from a young computer whiz from Ohio, named Jeremy Whisby. Until he met Geno, Jeremy struggled to find investors in his company so that he could bring his innovative gaming ideas into fruition as viable gaming products to be sold in retail stores. Geno happened to come across a news article on Jeremy online that talked about his fledgling company. The article peaked Geno's interest and he made contact with Jeremy because he always open new innovative investment opportunities.

The two men set up a meeting so Geno could view a demonstration of Jeremy's gaming software. Geno was genuinely impressed with what he saw. He offered Jeremy one million dollars in cash to become a silent majority partner in the company and to make it a subsidiary of the Caprese Foundation. Jeremy instantly agreed to the deal. The million dollars Geno offered was more money than he had ever saw in his young life and Geno convinced him he would make even more being his partner. Jeremy relocated the company to Baltimore and the rest was history. The company now had two video games on the market that did extremely well, earning close to thirty million dollars in profits in their first year. Jeremy had several more games to be released in the near future.

Every one of Geno's employees and partners had their own executive sized office suite within which to work and received a hefty salary for their efforts. He also made sure his staff had the best retirement plan available in the marketplace. He even gave them a generous employer matching contribution to their individual retirement accounts to ensure they would all be in a comfortable financial position once they decided to retire. Geno was generous and took care of his staff because he believed that if he treated them right, then they would give him their maximum effort in keeping his foundation running smoothly.

His brothers, Silvio and Cesare, were his silent partners in the foundation. They had no involvement whatsoever in the daily operations because Geno felt it was best they kept their distance from the legal side of the family business. Besides, neither of them had the patience or business savvy to be of any value to the foundation in a manner which could help it to grow financially. Silvio was a good earner in the streets and Geno needed him to continue to bring in the dirty money that he would, in turn, launder through various banking institutions, and use as financial capital for his legitimate business ventures. Cesare, on the other hand, was still a lost soul in life and he had no real interest in being a part of any big business deals. As long as Geno gave both of them a hefty check every month, neither one of them complained about their arrangement. Geno was free to do as he pleased in running things on his own without their interference.

Over the years, Geno wisely invested some of his large six and seven figure civil settlement checks and the lofty attorney fees that he collected from his clients into a host of profitable business corporations. He opened up a string of twenty-four hour laundromats that were dispersed throughout the city which brought in millions of dollars in revenue for the corporation. He wisely invested in the Cheddars Restaurant franchise to open up several locations in both Baltimore City and Baltimore County. He used his sharp negotiating skills to convince the traditionally closed circle of franchise owners to let him become a corporate partner in the profitable franchise. The foundation had substantial real estate holdings. They owned office buildings that leased office space to many small business owners. He had high end condominium rental properties in suburban communities, as well as income sensitive housing in the poorer sections of Baltimore City.

Geno was in the process of having a strip mall built in the heart of West Baltimore that would provide jobs for many poverty stricken inner city residents. The foundation owned a controlling interest in a chain of AMC movie theaters. Geno also opened up an exclusive car dealership located in the upscale Anne Arundel county area which catered to a population that paid top dollar for classic exotic sports cars. With all of these business ventures in tow, the Caprese Foundation was the definition of a diversified conglomerate business structure.

On this particular day, Geno was in his office late going over some case notes for a civil suit trial that he had in the morning. In the case, his client, Francis Mayweather, sued her former employer for wrongful termination. Ms. Mayweather was a drug counselor at a federally funded substance abuse treatment provider and she claimed her direct supervisor and the program director fired her after she was accused by a male client of being involved with him in an intimate sexual relationship. She denied the allegation vehemently, but they fired her anyway. They believed the client's assertion that she engaged in inappropriate sexual conduct with him despite the fact the patient had no proof to substantiate his claim other than his own account of their relationship. Ms. Mayweather asserted she was denied due process according to the program's own guidelines before she was fired. She was also unable to obtain another job since her termination because of the terms of her dismissal from her prior employer.

After reviewing the program's protocol with respect to patient complaints, Geno believed her case had merit and was one he could easily win. By the time he was done with the program in court, he was sure he would win Ms. Mayweather a nice mid, six figure settlement for her lost wages and the long term detrimental impact of her wrongful termination on her chances of finding a new job. He was going over the fine details of the case to make sure there were no flaws in his game plan.

Even though he did his best to busy himself with work, his mind still reflected back on his recent run-in with Nesta. He wasn't afraid, but cautious because Nesta was a dangerous man with an axe to grind. He knew that his rejection of his desire to be his business partner bruised his ego more than anything. He wondered why Nesta had not yet acted upon the veiled threat he made. Men like Nesta always resorted to violence to get what they wanted because it was in their nature. Geno had his whole team on high alert. While he usually walked around the city alone, he now traveled around flanked by two of his soldiers for extra security and protection. He wore a bulletproof vest under his suit. He had extra men around for security at his home for Carina and his children. He didn't tell Carina about what was going on, because she didn't need to know. He tried to act as normally as possible despite the fact that a war could pop off at any moment.

Geno took a break from working to clear his thoughts. He put his feet up on his desk to relax. His mind drifted off to several other business ideas he had in mind. He was interrupted out of his trance by a knock at his office door. The knock surprised him because it was close to seven in the evening and he thought all of his staff had already left for the day. He instructed the person to come in. Seconds later, in walked his personal assistant, Jia Maxim. She was a pretty, half Chinese and half Black beauty with a vibrant smile and bubbly personality. She was in her last year of her undergraduate studies at Towson State University as a Business Administration major.

"Jia, what are you still doing here?" he asked her. Her normal hours were from nine in the morning until five in the evening.

"I was just finishing up my notes from the big meeting you had the other day. I wanted to make sure I didn't miss any important details," she replied.

"I appreciate that, Jia, but it's late and you should be home enjoying your evening instead of being cooped up in this office," Geno suggested.

"It's not a problem at all. To be honest with you, I am almost as excited as you are to see this business venture come into fruition. I'm honored to be a part of something this major," she admitted humbly.

Jia had a look on her face like a young woman who was smitten with her much older, yet attractive mentor. Truth be told, she had a crush on Geno since the day she first met him and it only grew stronger the more she got to know him. She was fascinated by his intelligence and his powerful persona. Geno had no clue she felt that way about him.

"Yes, I will agree, this venture will be my crowning achievement if I can pull it off," Geno sat back and imagined.

The meeting he had the other day was with a group of investors he pulled together for his biggest and most significant business venture to date. He wanted to make a bid to buy the Los Angeles Clippers professional basketball from its disgraced owner, Donald Sterling, after he was fined two and a half million dollars and banned for life from the league by new NBA commissioner, Adam Silver, for recorded racist comments he made about NBA legend, Magic Johnson, and African Americans in general to his girlfriend, V. Stiviano. Sterling's comments caused a media frenzy and uproar in the African American community that put him in a position to have to sell the team, albeit against his will. When Geno saw the scandal on the news, his mind got to clicking. He saw dollars signs and more dollar signs. He instantly put a plan in motion to try to become the team's new owner. This was the big deal he had in the works that Nesta wanted to get in on. He wondered who among his investors leaked the information to him.

Geno didn't care that the team was located in Los Angeles. With the amount of money he stood to make as an NBA owner, he would relocate his family if necessary. He knew it would be easy work to convince Carina to fully support the move because she went along with whatever he wanted to do. As for his children, he found it hard to believe they would have a hard time adjusting to the beautiful California weather. He needed all of the pieces to the puzzle to fall into place perfectly to pull this deal off.

He estimated that it would cost at least a billion dollars to buy the team. The foundation didn't have that amount of capital alone so it was necessary for him to seek out investors who had money and shared a similar vision as he did. With the potential investment group he compiled, he planned to be the majority owner, with a fifty-one percent ownership stake, while the rest of the shares were equally dispersed amongst the five wealthy philanthropists he wanted to bring in on the deal. This was a can't miss business opportunity in his eyes and he felt that he had just as good a chance as any other investment group that put in a bid to buy the team. If he were able to pull this off, Geno would have exceeded even his wildest dreams and those of his father. Leonardo would definitely be proud of him to say the least. His brothers would surely be jealous of his success, as they always were, but he could care less. The power he would possess as a member of the elite club of NBA team owners would serve to cement his legacy. If he were successful, he would also have to sever all ties with the illegal activities he was engaged in with Silvio and his crew. He would offer them an opportunity to join him, but if they didn't agree to do so, he planned to go at it alone and hand over his stake in their illicit business activities to them totally.

"I am fully confident you will pull it off because the one thing I've learned about you Geno is you always get what you want," Jia stated confidently. The way she looked at him with lust in her eyes, he could have her right now if it was what he desired. Her panties were soaking wet from the thought of Geno on top of her.

"Well, thank you for your vote of confidence. Maybe I will take you with me to persuade the others to invest with me because you make such a compelling argument. However, for now, I want you to get out of here and go home. That's an order. Have one of the security guards walk you to your car because it's dangerous out in the streets this time of night."

"Okay, I will. I just have to shut my computer down before I leave. I hope you go home soon and get some rest too."

It made her feel warm inside he was concerned about her safety. Jia wished he wasn't married and she could tell him how she really felt about him. However, Carina and his children were a reality she couldn't ignore. She was reminded of this fact every time she saw the large painting of them Geno had done that hung in his office.

As Jia exited his office with a big smile on her face, Geno observed her backside. His eyes liked the way her body swayed in her form fitting skirt. She was a fine young tender thing, but he refused to indulge his lustful desires because he had to remain focused on running his business empire. In addition, he had a wife and two children at home. It had been years since he stepped out on Carina and ever since the last time he did, he made a conscious effort to not give in to temptation. He didn't want history to repeat itself. He got back to reviewing his case notes because it was the safe thing for him to do.

Chapter 17

"Help me, please! Don't let me die, please! Help me!" Princess pleaded with Cesare.

"Shut your mouth. Just shut up! This is all your fault. Why did you have to do this? Why?" Cesare rambled nervously.

He felt trapped inside of a bad movie. Princess's words played over and over inside of his head. Those were the last words he heard her speak before she ceased breathing. When he saw her eyes close, he checked her pulse to confirm she was dead. His ride or die chick was gone. Tears streamed down his cheeks. He felt emotionally distraught and empty inside. He couldn't believe that such a random twist of fate would turn his life upside down so fast.

Cesare paced back and forth in his apartment and cursed out loud at himself. He didn't understand how things went so far to the left so fast for him. One minute he was in bed with Princess about to have sex and the next minute, he stood over top of her with a bloody knife in his hand. Her body was lifeless. He couldn't believe what just happened. His home was now a bloody crime scene and he would be the main suspect once the police discovered Princess's dead body. Not knowing what to do, he called his best friend, Rah, and told him he needed him to get over to his house right away because it was an emergency. He didn't give him any details. Rah said he would be there shortly.

Princess and Cesare met one night he and Rah were hanging out at a nightclub in downtown Baltimore. She was out with her girls partying to celebrate her birthday. A dark skinned beauty, Princess resembled Naturi Naughton, the actress who played the role of rapper Lil' Kim in the movie about the Notorious B.I.G.'s life. She always had a thing for White guys ever since she was in high school because that was all she was around most of the time where she grew up at in Harford County. All of her girlfriends were either White or biracial. Her parents were the average middle class African American family. Her father worked as a Human Resource Administrator for the state of Maryland and her mother was a dental hygienist in a small dental practice in the Towson area of Baltimore County. They grew up in the suburbs, but Princess and her girls were into bad boys or the thug type of guys. That was why they loved to hang out in Baltimore City. They loved to party, smoke weed, and pop E pills. She was attracted to Cesare's flashy style and was even more turned on when he told her that he was a member of the Caprese crime family. Their relationship got hot and heated in no time and they wound up moving in together after just dating for six months.

From the very beginning, their relationship was a rocky one. They both were hot headed with a mean streak. They fought constantly about little things. Their life together was a roller coaster ride filled with a lot of drugs, violence, and wild sex. Princess started the fights just as much as Cesare did. Their kind of love was just as dangerous as it was fun. Their neighbors called the police on them a gang of times when they got into one of their heated exchanges.

This particular night started off rather calm when Cesare came home after a long day of supposedly working at Lila's. He actually did more drinking and flirting with the girls than working to be quite honest. He was drunk from all of the Tequila shots he downed and high from all of the marijuana he had smoked throughout the night. The liquor and weed had him extra horny by the time he left the club for the night.

While he was at Lila's earlier in the evening, he had already had sex with one of the girls in the VIP lounge, but that wasn't enough for him.

He was still in the mood to go another round when he got home. Consequently, he made his way to their bedroom and found Princess asleep. She was stretched out across their bed with nothing but a thong on. The sight of her firm, round butt was all it took to get him aroused. Cesare quickly disrobed and climbed into bed with Princess. He started to kiss her on the back of her neck because he knew that was her Achilles' heel. It worked like a charm. In no time at all, the moisture began to form in her sweet spot. He grinded his penis up against her backside for a few minutes while his hand disappeared in between her thighs.

His fingers fit snugly inside of her vagina and he managed to get her more excited every time he moved them in and out of her. While he finger fucked her, he planted wet kisses all over the sides of her neck. He whispered in her ear all of the nasty things he planned to do to her body tonight. Sleep was no longer on her mind. She was eager to experience the pain and pleasure he intended to give her. He sucked on her breasts to increase her anxiety. Before she let him penetrate her, she needed to get a taste of his penis inside of her mouth. She wasted no time in wrapping her full lips around his manhood to swallow it whole. While she went to work, she noticed a strange odor that permeated from his crotch area. It was the scent of sweat mixed with another woman's cheap perfume.

Princess asked him if was he with another woman and he nonchalantly admitted he was. However, he said she didn't mean anything to him because it was just sex and nothing more. She was pissed off, but didn't let her anger show right away. She wasn't upset just because he cheated on her, but she was more livid he didn't even have the decency to wear a condom or to even take a shower afterwards before he tried to have sex with her. The last thing she wanted to do was to be swapping body fluids with some random chick that could have God knows what venereal disease between her thighs.

Princess wanted Cesare to feel every ounce of her anger. She didn't say a word, but just calmly let go of his penis, got up out of the bed, and walked out of the bedroom into the kitchen area. She returned to the bedroom with a large knife in her hand ready to do damage. Cesare instantly sobered up. When she lunged at him with the knife, he was able to move out the way in just enough to time to avoid getting stabbed. He managed to get to his feet and to make it out of the bedroom without being cut by the large blade in her hand. Princess was hot on his trail. They both ran through the house butt naked. She chased him all around their house and when she felt that she was close enough, she took another swipe at him, only to just miss.

Cesare made the mistake of trying to run into the bathroom. Princess was strong enough

171

to apply enough force to push the door open before it was fully closed. The force with which she pushed the door propelled Cesare up against the bathroom wall. She swung the knife at him again, but this time when he blocked the knife away, it swung back in her direction and plunged into her chest. Princess was shocked when she looked down to see she accidentally stabbed herself. The rapid loss of blood made her light headed and she fell backward onto the floor into the hallway area.

Out of sheer instinct, Cesare pulled the knife out of her chest and the blood began to flow even faster. Not sure what to do, he grabbed a towel out of the linen closet and pressed it up against her wound to try and stop the blood flow. It didn't work. Princess cursed and screamed at him to help her, but he didn't know what else to do. He held her in his arms and rocked her back and forth. He wasn't into religion, but he prayed to God harder than he ever did before in his life that God could work a miracle and save Princess. However, it was too late. He realized this when her body began to feel cold.

In a panic, Cesare laid her gently on the floor and ran into the bathroom to take a shower to wash all of her blood off of him. Once he was done, he threw the clothes that he wore all day back on and planned to make his exit out of the back door. Before he left out, he grabbed the knife off the floor and threw it inside of his book bag. He took one last look at Princess before he walked out of the back door. Just as he made his way down the stairs, he saw Rah pull up. He ran toward the car at a rapid pace. Once he reached the car, he opened up the passenger door and climbed in.

"What the hell happened, Cesare?" Rah asked him. Rah noticed the disheveled state his friend was in. He was used to Cesare getting into brawls with Princess and him having to come over to intervene between the two of them. However, tonight was different. Cesare was in a somber mood and looked spaced out. He pulled off so that they could talk while he drove down the road with no particular destination in mind.

"Man, everything happened so fast. It all seemed like a dream. One minute we were in bed about to get it on and then she stops going down on me to tell me that she smelled another woman's perfume on me. The next thing I know, she is coming at me with a big ass knife and chasing me around the house. I pushed her arm away when she swung the knife at me, but when I did; the knife went into her chest and killed her. Princess is dead! She's dead, Rah," Cesare explained in an emotional state.

"It was an accident, but I'm going to get you through this situation, my brother," Rah stated calmly. He shook his head in disbelief that he found himself in the midst of Cesare's relationship drama once again.

"I need you to say I was with you after I left the club. I need an alibi. That way the police will think it was a robbery and somebody tried to rape her when they broke in," Cesare suggested. He felt bad that Princess was dead, but he wasn't trying to go to jail because of such an unfortunate accident.

"I got you. Stop worrying yourself, Mon," Rah assured him.

"I also need you to get rid of the knife for me," Cesare requested

"I'll take care of it for you. Reach in the ashtray and take a few pulls off of that good ganja to ease your mind," Rah suggested.

"I appreciate you, fam," Cesare replied. He was relieved that Rah had his back.

He used Rah's lighter, which was in the center console, to light the already half smoked blunt. He put it to his lips and inhaled the fumes. It gave him just the escape he needed at the moment. After he got a good night's sleep, he would think about his next move. He had to lay low for a while because he was sure the police would want to question him about how Princess died given that the house was in his name. Once everything hit the fan, it was just a matter of time before Geno found out and gave him hell for messing up once again. He could hear him now telling him how stupid he was which, was the last thing he needed to hear. Princess's death was truly an accident and not his fault. Sadly, Geno wouldn't see it that way. He would look at is as another blemish on the Caprese family name and another mess he would have to clean up.

Chapter 18

"Hey, Marietta, how about you get up off your butt and answer that door. It's Geno. Don't keep my boy waiting out there," Leonardo yelled from the bedroom. Today wasn't a good day for him. He was in so much pain he couldn't get out of the bed. He took the pain medication the doctor prescribed for him, but it did little to alleviate his suffering.

"Shut your yapper, old man. I'm getting the door," she replied. She was busy in the kitchen washing dishes. She dried her hands off and made her way to the front door to open it for Geno.

"Hey, is that Sophia Loren? What did you do with my Mama?"

"Stop kidding around, you smooth talker you. Sophia Loren wished she did look as good as me. Get in here. Let me take a look at you.

You're looking kind of thin. Has that daughter in law of mine been feeding you?"

"Yes, she feeds me just fine, Ma. I'm just stressed and have a lot on my mind is all. Don't worry about me. I'll be okay. I hope that old man of mine knows how lucky of a guy he is to have a beautiful gal like you to call his own."

"Thank you, son. At least one of my sons knows how to make his mother feel good about herself."

Silvio and Cesare rarely came by to see them these days. They were too busy living their own lives to take time out for their parents. Marietta was hurt by the fact she didn't see them too often. She carried them both in her womb and took care of them like a mother was supposed to do while Leonardo earned out in the streets, yet neither Silvio or Cesare could find the time to spend with her. Marietta had it rough caring for Leonardo all alone. At least she had her Geno to rely upon to help her out sometimes.

Geno came by as often as he could despite the challenges presented by his busy schedule. He would sit up with his father for hours on end and watch sports or get history lessons from the stories he told him about his encounters with notorious gangsters from the past in the streets of New York. Geno soaked up all of the knowledge he could from his old man. He didn't understand why his brothers were so ungrateful and jealous of him and his relationship with their parents, but he didn't care. He would be there for both of them for as long as they were here on this Earth.

"So what is the important business that Pops wants to talk to me about?"

"I'll let him explain it to you. He's upstairs in the bedroom. Go on up there."

His father had called him several times in the past week and said he wanted to speak with him about something that was on his mind. They always had an open line of communication between them. Geno often sought his father's sagely advice whenever he had a tough business decision to make. There was a lot of wisdom in that old brain of his from which Geno could extract good information he could put to use. Leonardo saw it all and did it all in his lifetime. He rubbed elbows with the most ruthless gangsters and politicians. He hung out with celebrity athletes and Hollywood actors and actresses. He had a keen ability to read people well enough to know their intentions before they acted them out. His gut instinct about someone was never wrong.

When Geno heard Leonardo's voice on the phone the last time they talked, he heard a troubling tone in his voice. He didn't sound like himself. That was why he made it his business to leave the office early today to stop by to see him. He needed to know what was wrong. When he reached the top of the stairs, he made a sharp right turn and headed toward his parents' bedroom. He entered the room to see his father coughing heavily and in a visibly weakened state.

"Pops, are you okay?"

"Hey, Geno, I'm fine. This Goddamn cancer is kicking my ass. Tell me something good, son. Make an old man smile."

"Well, Pops, you wouldn't believe what your son has cooking right now. Let's just say that you might be looking at the next owner of the Los Angeles Clippers right here!" Geno stated excitedly.

"You have got to be shitting me, son. That's a major power move. How the hell did you pull that off?"

"Well, I haven't pulled it off yet, but things are looking good. I just used the skills you taught me Pops to put the right people at the table to make it happen. You always told me the best business investment was to invest somebody else's money and let it make money for you."

"I taught you well, Son. I taught you well."

"Yeah, you did old man."

"Well, Geno, you and I have always been close unlike your brothers. They were always so hard headed, especially that Silvio. Even though he's your brother, I wouldn't tell him about this big business deal you've got going. He's always been jealous of you and I can see him trying to mess this deal up out of spite. As for Cesare, I swear I tell your mother all of the time I think we brought home the wrong baby. He smokes so much dope that his mind is fried. No son of mine should be on no damn drugs!" Leonardo stated with anger and conviction. He got a little excited and became short of breath. Geno did his best to calm him down.

"Breathe easy, Pops. You're not telling me something I don't already know about my brothers. Let me deal with them. You worry about your health. Is that all you wanted to talk to me about?" Geno asked.

Leonardo laid back on his pillow and let out a loud sigh. He'd put this conversation off for long enough. It was time for him to get it off of his chest so his conscious would be clear.

"No, it's not son. I've always tried to be straight with you so I'ma just lay this out to you and let the chips fall where they may. Before you pass judgment, at least hear me out. When you and Silvio were teenagers and Cesare was just a baby, your mother and I were going through a rough patch in our marriage when I met this beautiful Black girl by the name of Raylene Jones. I think you know I love your mother more than life itself, but I'm a man first and I've always had a weakness for a beautiful woman with a nice set of legs. I know you've had your share of side flings through the years, but it didn't make you any less of a man, did it?" Leonardo asked.

"I've done my share of dirt in the past, but I'm faithful to my wife today. Okay, so you had an affair with a Black woman over twenty years ago. What does that have to do with anything going on today, Pops?" he asked. Geno thought his father might be in the early stages of dementia to tell him about a side girlfriend from his past.

"Well, it was more than just a fling, son. Our affair lasted for years. She and I were in love. I loved her and your mother at the same time. I played around and got myself caught up. When she found out I was married, she cut me off completely and wanted nothing to do with me. She was a proud woman. What I'm trying to tell you son is that you have a brother and sister that you have never met," Leonardo finally blurted out. Geno's face turned red. He stared at him and was speechless for a moment.

"Pops, tell me that you didn't just say I have two siblings that you had by another woman over twenty something years ago and I'm just finding out about this? This has to be a joke, right?" Geno inquired in a state of confusion. His mental equilibrium was thrown off keel. His mind was blown. The tone of the conversation totally shifted in a negative direction.

"It's not a joke, son. It's the truth. I've been holding this in all of this time because your mother made me promise that I would never tell you boys. She was embarrassed and felt ashamed because of what I did. I didn't want to go to my grave with you not knowing. Your brother's name is Jericho and your sister's name is Shavon," Leonardo uttered as he continued his confession. He felt relieved to have gotten this secret off of his chest.

"So you had two families that you took care of at the same time? How did I not catch wind of this when I was growing up? You had us around you all of the time," Geno uttered. He was bewildered.

"No, son, you weren't with me all of the time. Remember, your father is a very crafty man. I know how to be incognito when I need to be. As for me taking care of two families, that didn't happen. I wanted to provide for Jericho and Shavon, but their mother wouldn't let me. She threatened to call the police on me every time I came around. You know in our line of work, that's not a good idea. Even though she tried to stop me from seeing my children, I still kept tabs on them in my own way. She died a few years back in a bad fire. Jericho and Shavon were raised by her grandparents who couldn't stand me because I was Italian. Racism was a big thing at the time. They wouldn't let me anywhere near my kids. My hands were tied. I was able to find out quite a bit about them over the years though. Jericho, well son, let's just say he is definitely a Caprese by nature. He is definitely cut from the same mold as us and would fit right in with you and Silvio. As for Shavon, she's been through a lot. I'm telling you all of this because I want you all to have a chance to get to know one another," Leonardo confessed. Being near death had a way of making a man want to right some of his past wrongs.

"You no good son of a bitch, I can't believe you did this to my mother. I can't even imagine what she has felt like all of these years because of you. I hate you with all of my heart and I would kill you, but the cancer is doing a good job of that on its own. You're a piece of shit!" Geno yelled at Leonardo while he stormed out of the room. He ran down the steps and out of the front door, without even saying a word to his mother. The man he looked up to all of his life as being a stand up guy had let him down in a major way. He needed to clear his head to be able to properly process the bombshell news.

Chapter 19

It took a several days before Princess's body was found by the police. Her mother, Lena, grew concerned when she hadn't heard from her in three days. That was unusual because they communicated either on the phone or on Facebook at least twice a day. When she called her phone, she didn't get an answer and she never opened any of the Facebook inbox messages she sent her. Lena called Cesare's phone and he didn't pick up either. She never liked him and always told Princess he was bad news. When Lena couldn't even reach Cesare, her concern turned into fear that something bad had happened to her. She decided to drive into the city to her house to see for herself what was going on with her daughter and to find out why she hadn't heard from her.

When Lena arrived at their house, she knocked on the door, but got no response. She remembered Princess told her she and Cesare kept a spare key under the flower pot on the front porch. Lena found the key and let herself in the house.

Lena wasn't prepared for what she encountered once she was inside. The strong odor from Princess's dead body hit her as soon as she opened the door. She almost threw up instantly. She prayed what she suspected wasn't true, but the smell of death was a scent not to be confused with anything else. To confirm her suspicion, she put her hand over her mouth and nose to block out the pungent aroma as she made her way inside. She grew lightheaded and her heart began to race when she saw the blood all over the floor in the hallway. Lena lost all control when she saw Princess's lifeless naked body sprawled out in front of the hallway bathroom. Tears streamed down her cheeks as she dropped to the floor to hold what was left of her baby girl. She rocked her back and forth in her arms and prayed that she wasn't dead, but she knew better. Princess was gone. A nervous wreck, Lena managed to summon up the resolve to call the police.

When the police arrived, they instantly sealed off the crime scene and went to work. Lena, in a highly emotional state, instantly placed the blame on Cesare for her daughter's death. She told the police he was violent and that he and her daughter fought constantly. When she gave the police officer his full name, it instantly caught his attention. The name Caprese had that effect on law enforcement officers. Anybody with that last name was a public enemy in the eyes of the police force. They all had a hard on for them and wanted to see the entire family rot in jail, especially Geno. The police particularly detested him because of all of the police brutality and misconduct lawsuits he won against them.

During their investigation of the crime scene, they determined that Princess died from a single knife wound to the chest. However, they were unable to locate the knife that killed her. They also didn't detect any signs of forced entry to indicate that Princess might have been attacked during a robbery attempt. Most of the time it meant the victim knew the perpetrator intimately and willingly let him into the residence. The fact that Princess was naked lent credence to this theory and also suggested her death may have resulted from some form of lover's quarrel that erupted into a brutally violent confrontation.

With Cesare nowhere to be found to explain his side of the story, he looked more guilty than innocent. Based upon her body temperature, the crime scene investigator indicated that she had been dead for several days. That made Cesare even more suspect because it seemed suspicious that he hadn't been home in that time frame to discover the body. To find him was their top priority. An APB was put out for his arrest. He was considered to be armed and dangerous. It was broadcast on all of the local news stations and Cesare's picture was flashed across the screen for all to see.

The police officers did their best to console Lena, but nothing could adequately comfort a mother who discovered her child's dead body. She was devastated to say the least. She wanted answers to so many questions. She didn't understand what her daughter did to deserve to die. She wanted justice and for somebody to suffer for her loss. That somebody in her mind was Cesare. Her nerves were shot and she began to hyperventilate. One of the female police officers accompanied her to the hospital to get checked out. As for Cesare, he was a wanted man. He could only hide for so long before the law caught up with him. The sad part about this situation was Cesare was actually innocent, but it didn't matter. The police department had a member of the Caprese family in its scope.

Chapter 20

Geno's head was still spinning after the surprise news his father dropped on him. He was usually a clear headed thinker, but this situation had him at a loss. He honestly didn't know what to think or feel. He wanted to hate Leonardo, but the love he had for him made it difficult. He tried his best to see the situation from his vantage point, but found it hard to do. He couldn't fathom himself fathering a child, even as a result of an affair, and not taking care of his child. It just wasn't in Geno's character to not be a stand up guy. It was how his father always taught him to be, but as fate would have it, Leonardo couldn't live up to his own standards he set for his sons. Geno saw him as a hypocrite and a liar. He told himself that for Leonardo to have cancer slowly take away his life was a fitting punishment for his betrayal of his own family. He felt no guilt at all for feeling this way. He never wanted to speak to him again in life. When he died, he didn't want to attend his funeral to say his final goodbyes. As far as he was concerned, Leonardo Caprese was already dead to him.

What pissed Geno off the most was that he could only imagine how much of a burden this placed on his mother. To know that your husband got another woman pregnant with two children had to crush her emotionally and mentally, yet she never let it show to them not one bit all of these years. The lack of respect he now felt for his father was replaced by the greater respect and appreciation he now had for his mother. She was even more flawless now in his eyes. Leonardo didn't deserve such an elegant and loyal woman in his life. Any other woman would have left him after she found out about the depths of his infidelity. Instead, Marietta stayed around and raised her children. She was a soldier. She was his real hero.

As for his newly discovered siblings, Jericho and Shavon, he felt no ill feelings toward them. It wasn't their fault they shared a father who was a piece of shit. He found himself wanting to know more about them. He didn't care that they were African American because racism had no place in his heart. He already had John Lucci on the case to try and locate them. From what Leonardo said about Jericho he evidently was involved in the street life in some capacity. He needed to see to what extent. Geno hoped he would be able to develop some form of a relationship with them over time. He had such a distant and dysfunctional relationship with Silvio and Cesare that any form of sibling comradery would be a welcome addition to his life.

Over the past few days, Carina could tell that something was wrong with Geno, but he acted like everything was fine. She was his best friend and he confided in her with his most intimate thoughts, but he wasn't ready to share this news with her just yet. The time wasn't right for him to spring the news on her that she had two new in-laws and their children had an aunt and uncle that just came out of nowhere. He didn't quite have a handle on how he felt about it all himself and until he did, he felt it was best to let the situation marinate for awhile. Once he heard back from Lucci, he would decide how to best proceed.

To take his mind off of that situation, Geno had just finished up another intense kickboxing training session with his personal trainer, Rico, in his personal gym located in the basement of his home. He was drenched in his own sweat. He started taking classes with Rico a few months ago. He tried it out because he wanted to find a new way to get in some beneficial cardiovascular exercise besides just running on a treadmill. Kickboxing not only helped him to stay in shape, but also allowed for him to sharpen his mental focus. The high level of stress that he experienced with all of the professional demands placed upon him as the boss of so many business ventures significantly decreased since they began their training sessions. He planned to stick with this routine for a quite some time until something else came along to peak his interest.

"So, how did I do? Am I ready to be the Italian Bruce Lee or what?" Geno joked with Rico while he packed up his belongings. A black belt in Brazilian jiu jitsu, Rico saw potential in his star pupil.

"You're hand-eye coordination has definitely improved since we first started working out together. Your speed is improving as well. I'm definitely impressed with your progress thus far, but we have a long way to go," Rico replied. He made it a point to not praise his students too much because he didn't want their egos to make them lose focus on perfecting their craft and technique.

"Well, I'm open to learning everything you can teach me. So are we on for next Thursday at the same time?" Geno asked.

"Yes, indeed, your appointment is locked in for six o'clock in the evening," Rico confirmed after he looked at his calendar on his Ipad. Rico shook Geno's hand and then made his exit out of the basement door.

Once Rico was gone, Geno hopped in the shower in the full sized basement bathroom to freshen up. When he got out of the shower, he threw on a pair of shorts and a t-shirt and headed upstairs to have dinner with his family. Even though he was an extremely busy man with a lot of people who demanded his time and attention, Geno made it a point to be home early enough from work at least three times a week to be able to eat dinner with Carina and the children. Their family time was an important part of his life. Carina and his children reminded him why he worked so hard. They served as his foundation and primary motivation for his desire to be the man that he was. When he made his way upstairs, Carina, Gianna, and Stefan were seated at the dinner table.

"Something smells good in here. What are we eating tonight?" Geno asked while he took his seat at the head of the dinner table.

"We're having Chicken marsala, whole green beans sautéed with sweet peppers, and Caesar salad. We waited for you so that you can bless the table," Carina replied.

"Come on, Daddy, please just say a prayer so we can eat," Stefan begged.

The food looked good and he was starving. Stefan was ready to fix himself a plate and tear into the hearty meal. He was a growing boy with a stomach that was a bottomless pit. On the flip side, Gianna ate very little because she wanted to make sure she maintained her slim figure so she was in top shape for her budding modeling career.

"Our father who is Heaven, please bless this food we are about to eat. You have blessed us to be able to live a good life and have the best of everything. I thank you for it all on behalf of me and my family. Amen."

After Geno finished his prayer, they all got down to the business of devouring the delicious meal Carina had prepared. Geno ate until he was stuffed. Stefan had three helpings of lasagna before his little belly was full. When they were all done with their food, Carina cleaned off the table and placed the dishes in the dishwasher. Stefan and Gianna made a quick beeline for their bedrooms so they could get on their Ipads before it was time for them to go to bed because they had school in the morning. Geno and Carina retired to the family room to snuggle and watch a movie. They were interrupted when Gianna ran into the room in a frantic state.

"Daddy, OMG, you have got to see this! You will not believe this!"

"What is it, honey?"

"It's Uncle Cesare. He's on the news!"

Geno jumped up so fast he almost knocked Carina to the floor. Gianna handed him her Ipad so he could see what got her in such an uproar. Geno's whole facial expression changed when he saw the composite photo of Cesare on the front page of the local news station's web page. The news article talked about Princess being stabbed to death and implicated Cesare as the leading suspect. The story stated that the police apprehended him coming out of a friend's apartment. Geno couldn't believe his eyes. He knew his brother was an idiot, but he wasn't a murderer. He had to have been set up he surmised. He handed Gianna her Ipad back when he was done with the article.

"I've got to go see what's going on with Cesare. I'll be back!" Geno stated before he made his abrupt departure.

Carina wasn't upset that their quality time was interrupted. She understood. Cesare was family. As for Geno, he was already stressed out dealing with the Nesta situation, his father's recent revelation about his love children, and now this situation had to come along. He felt like somebody had to have put a curse on him to have to deal with so much drama at one time.

Chapter 21

Detective Elvin Swift had been on the Baltimore City Police department for eight years. He was in the Homicide division for the past three. In his mid thirties, he stood an even five feet and eleven inches tall and weighed closed to one hundred and eighty pounds. He wore his hair cut close and had a thick goatee. He was often mistaken for the actor Michael Jai White. He loved the comparison because it helped him get many ladies throughout the years. He lived alone in a small one bedroom apartment in the city. He didn't have any children or a wife, but had several females he dated. His job was his full-time commitment.

Swift was one of the most decorated officers on the force because his rate of case closures stayed in the high ninety percent range every year. His investigation skills were impeccable. Whenever he had a hunch about a suspect, he went with it and was usually right. When he saw the physical evidence against Cesare, it just didn't seem to gel with him. Also, after he talked with him, he studied his body language and got the vibe that he didn't have the heart of a killer, even if it were a crime of passion. Cesare seemed too soft hearted to be capable of murder. He did, however, sense that he knew what happened to Princess, but was afraid to talk. He could see the fear of jail in his eyes and hoped he could use it against him to make him break down. Swift decided to take one more crack at Cesare to see if he could get some information out of him before his attorney arrived. He walked back into the interrogation room where Cesare was being held to try his hand one more time.

"I ain't saying a thing until I talk to my lawyer, pig. You're wasting your time. I want my one phone call," Cesare spit at him as soon as he saw Swift enter the room. Cesare was entitled to one phone call, but they hadn't let him make it yet. They wanted to let him stew for a bit to see if he might confess. Cesare held his own thus far. He refused to crack.

"You'll have plenty of time to call your attorney. Right now, how about you and I have a little conversation, Cesare. Your last name is Caprese, right? We've had you guys under investigation for years. Your brother is the legendary Geno Caprese? Everybody knows about him. He walks around town like he's a big bad business executive when he's really just a thug dressed in an expensive suit. He ain't no joke. Neither is your other brother, Silvio. He's a straight killer. I haven't been able to pin a murder charge on him yet though. You come from a long line of certified gangsters. I know it must be hard on you to walk in their shadows all of these years, huh?" he asked. Swift attempted to get a rise out Cesare in hopes it would get him to talk, but Cesare remained defiant.

"That's right, pig. My family runs this city. You better recognize. When my brother is done with you, you'll be working security at Lexington Market," Cesare shot back cockily.

"Yeah, your brothers are some serious cats, but you, on the other hand, the streets don't respect you because you haven't put in any work. My CI's out there say you're the weak link in the Caprese family. I hear that you're the one brother that can't carry his own weight. I bet it sucks to be you, huh?"

"Fuck you, pig. I can hold my own. Try me and see how I get down. My brothers don't have to carry nothing for me. I'm just trying to do me with this music thing. When you see me on MTV, don't get mad when your girl gets all wet watching me rock the mic," Cesare blurted out. He was clearly delusional because he still held onto the fantasy that he would make it as a rap star.

Swift laughed at his rant. His words struck a nerve with Cesare because his words were true. Cesare was the black sheep of the family. Everything he did, he messed up and Geno had to always come behind him and make the situation right. It frustrated Cesare to no end. That's why he stayed high all of the time to escape the frustration from his constant failures.

"You want to be a rapper? You've got to be kidding me, right? You do know that you're a White boy and that the White boy quota for rappers has been filled up by Eminem, Yelawolf, and Machine Gun Kelly, don't you? You need to let that pipe dream go, fella," Swift further antagonized him. Cesare flared up and looked like he wanted to cry. His feelings were clearly hurt because Swift just crushed his dream.

"Go to hell, pig. You don't know me. You don't know my struggle. I'ma make it to be big time. You just watch," Cesare spoke with much less confidence than he had when they first started to talk. All of his life he was branded a failure and weak. He wanted respect, but did nothing to earn it the right way.

"I'm sorry for being hard on you, kid, but I'm trying to help you. I don't think you killed your girl, but I think you were there and know what happened. Why don't you tell me what really went down so I can see what I can do for you."

"I know I didn't do it because I haven't been home. I was with my boy Rah at his crib when she was killed. He already told you guys that. So why am I still here?"

"Well, I hate to disappoint you soldier, but your boy Rah is not co-signing that story. He says you two weren't together the last few days. You need to come up with a better alibi than that one."

"You're lying because Rah is my brother. He wouldn't do me like that ever. I don't believe you."

"I lie to you not, Cesare. We have no physical evidence to tie you to the murder scene. If you had an airtight alibi for the time that we believe Princess was killed, we would have been let you go. You're going to eat this murder charge if you don't tell me something."

Reality hit Cesare like a ton of bricks. Rah had crossed him, but he didn't understand why. Without his alibi, he was screwed. A murder charge would get him some serious time in jail and he wasn't cut out to do a long bid. He couldn't put up a front anymore. He began to shake like a leaf and tears poured from his eyes.

"I didn't kill her, man. You've got to believe me. It was an accident. That's the truth."

Before he could say another word, Geno entered the room in full attorney mode. He knew how the police tried to squirm a confession out of a suspect to make their job easier, but he wasn't about to let them do that to his little brother.

"C, shut your mouth. Don't say another word. Officer, I need you to leave the room. I need to talk to my client," Geno spoke angrily.

"By all means, he's all yours. I found out what I needed to know already," Swift bragged. He slyly grinned at Geno and walked out of the room.

"Pull yourself together, Cesare. Don't ever let these pigs see you crack. You're a Caprese so act like it for once. Tell me what happened."

Cesare felt relieved that Geno arrived when he did. He was on the verge of telling Swift the whole story about the night Princess died. Instead, he told it to Geno. When Geno heard his version of things, including how Rah double crossed him, he instantly came up with a defense strategy.

"So, what's going to happen to me now?" Cesare asked.

"If your story is true, then you have no worries. My subject matter experts can clearly show that the knife wound was self-inflicted. They're just trying to railroad you because they can't get a case against me or the family. Don't worry about a thing. I'll get you out of here."

"Thanks, Geno. I know I fuck up a lot, but if you get me out of this mess, I'ma do better. I swear I will."

"I hear you, kid. Just hold tight for me. Oh, by the way, the police didn't find the knife. Where is it?"

"I gave it to Rah. He was supposed to get rid of it for me."

"You did what? Cesare, dammit man. You never make things easy for me. I'll fix it, somehow. Just stay calm and let me do what I do. Hold your head up until I get you out of here. I love you little brother."

"I love you too, Geno."

Geno gave Cesare a hug and exited the interrogation room. He felt sorry for Cesare because he simply couldn't help himself. He just had bad luck with everything he did. Geno did his best to give him opportunities to be successful, but it just wasn't in him. He was beyond frustrated with him. He pulled out his phone to make a phone call he truly dreaded having to make. The phone rang, but he got no answer. He decided to leave a message.

"Nesta, this is Geno. It appears that we need to talk. I think that I may have something you might want and vice versa. Give me a call when you get this message."

Cesare had no clue how big of a mistake he made. He put a crucial piece of evidence that could affect his freedom in the hands of the son of a man that Geno was about to potentially go to war with soon. When Geno found out Rah backed out of giving Cesare an alibi, he already knew what the deal was. Nesta clearly had the upper hand right now, but not for long. Geno mastered the art of pulling the Ace of Spades out of nowhere.

Chapter 22

Rah felt no guilt at all about betraying Cesare. It was nothing personal, but strictly business. When he picked Cesare up the night Princess died, he had the best intentions of being a supportive friend to help him out of a bad situation. He had helped Cesare out of a jam more times than he could count in the past. Truthfully, he felt sorry for him because he couldn't win for losing. He was just cursed with bad luck. Even when Cesare had good intentions, things always went bad for him somehow. He was like a wounded bird that needed to be constantly watched over. Since they had become friends, Rah was that protector who had his back all of the time.

When Cesare gave him the knife that Princess accidentally stabbed herself with, initially he planned to get rid of it to help Cesare out. He also planned to say they were together the night she was killed to give him an alibi so he would be in the clear. However, after he thought about it for a minute, his mind shifted in another direction. He saw an opportunity to make something happen for himself and took advantage of the situation.

His father always taught him that the window for success for a Black men, either in the streets or in the legitimate world, was a small one and he had to be aggressive at all times to take advantage of every opportunity that presented itself. If he let his window of opportunity pass him by, he would be assured to live a mediocre existence. He also told him if a man doesn't take advantage of his window for success, someone else would swoop in and take right from up under his nose.

Nesta gave him these lessons out of his own personal experiences. He was living proof that a man had to either feast or be stricken by famine if he didn't stake a claim to what he believed was rightfully his. He lived his life by these principles and attributed his success to his obedience to this frame of mind. It was what separated him from the rest of the poor and downtrodden brothers who grew up with him in Jamaica. He wanted to one day be a rich man and he was willing to do whatever was necessary to make that happen. He didn't care if he had to kill his own brother or stab his best friend in the back. He wanted success at all costs. The vast wealth he now had was at a great cost, but, to him, it was all worth it because he got what he wanted.

Rah always strived to follow in his father's footsteps and lived his life to please him at every turn. It was just the two of them since his mother died. Nesta told him she died from childbirth complications after he was born. He said Rah was Jah's own personal blessing to him as a sign of greater things to come. When Rah was younger, he made no apologies for the ruthless criminal lifestyle he lived. He convinced him that every action he took was to build an empire as a legacy for Rah to carry on. Rah grew up in awe of the way men used to fear Nesta when he walked down the streets in their hometown in Jamaica. People would clear a pathway for him to walk down the street like he was Moses. He was Nesta Clarke's son and it made him feel proud to make that statement. He looked at himself as being from royalty.

Even though Nesta gave him whatever he wanted and spoiled him to no end, there was also a dark side to their relationship. Rah felt like he had to be perfect at all times. He had no room to make the same mistakes most teenagers made. If he ever came up short of his father's expectations, the punishment was harsh. For example, when he was around eight years old, he came to Nesta crying and told him about being picked on in school by another boy who was two years older than him. He said the boy beat him up regularly for no reason. He expected for Nesta to sympathize with him and be a source of comfort, but he got just the opposite. Nesta beat him and told him that crying and whining was for little girls. He demanded he go back and face the little boy and do whatever was necessary to gain his respect. He told him that if the boy was too big and strong for him to beat up with his fists, then he should be resourceful and grab a stick or rock to use to gain an advantage over him.

When Rah went back to school the next day and the boy picked on him out in the schoolyard, he took his pencil and stabbed the boy in the stomach. He grabbed a rock off the ground and bashed him upside the head. Blood spilled everywhere. The boy fell to the ground and Rah jumped on top of him to continue to administer a beat down. He didn't stop raining blows on the boy until several teachers pulled him off of the poor boy. His point was made. He gained a reputation among his classmates as a fearless fighter and they respected him. When he told his father what he did, Nesta was proud of him. He was relieved to have found favor with his father and hero. From that point on, he made a conscious effort to try and stay on Nesta's good side.

As his father's right hand man, he was well aware of his intentions to try and maneuver himself in a position to take over Geno's crew. He saw it coming from the first moment he told him he was friends with Cesare. In fact, Nesta asked him to get even closer to Cesare than he already was. Rah knew he had an angle because that was just how Nesta operated. His making peace with the Jackson brothers was just a means to end. It gave him an inroad to Geno and his vast world of power and influence. It set the stage for a grander scheme he concocted in his head.

Nesta was a Boss in his own right, but recognized Geno had a reach which superseded his own. He could make things happen that Nesta couldn't. With that in mind, Nesta sought to acquire Geno's powerful contacts and organization to make them his. He wanted to be the top dog and not share the spotlight with anyone. His ego wouldn't allow for that to happen. Truth be told, he had plans to eventually kill Liddell and take over his organization when it was all said and done. If his own cousin and flesh and blood wasn't safe from his cruel intentions, to go after Geno was par for the course.

Rah wanted desperately to solidify his position next to his father once his master plan went into full effect. He saw himself taking over the throne when the time was right. To prove his worth, he knew he had to provide Nesta with something substantial which would peak his interest. Cesare's misfortune gave him that something big he could use to achieve his goal. That was why he was on his way to see Nesta right now. He knew he would be pleased with the gift he was about to give him. He felt bad for betraying Cesare's friendship, but he had to do what he had to do for himself. It was a dog eat dog world out here and he planned to be the last pit bull standing.

Chapter 23

John Lucci used to be one of New York City's most decorated police officers, but he was far from an honorable man. A veteran of the force for over fifteen years, he was the epitome of what would be considered a dirty cop. He took bribes, shook down drug dealers for cash, fulfilled contract killings for the Mob, and committed a host of other crimes while he hid behind his badge. Rumor had it there were several contracts out on his life, but no one was able to kill him because Lucci was too smart and resourceful. He always stayed two steps ahead of everybody else.

Lucci's world came crashing down as a result of one fatal flaw he had: he loved to fool around with prostitutes. His fetish wound up costing him his job after he messed with the wrong one. The one that did him in was a sixteen year old call girl named Gloria. She worked for an escort agency he found online which was run by a Russian Madam named Malvina Azarov. She was a mean middle aged woman who used to be a hooker herself before she got too old to turn tricks. At that point, her pimp, Boris, whom also happened to be the father of her two children, made her his bottom bitch. She learned the prostitution game on another level. When Boris died a few years ago, she decided to go into business for herself and started her own escort agency. She now had over twenty girls in her stable. Gloria was able to work for her because she lied about her age and verified it with a fake ID.

Lucci was a loner and didn't have much time for a relationship so he preferred to just pay hookers for sex whenever he felt horny. He had no idea Malvina's agency, which was located in Newark, New Jersey, was under police investigation for months. One night when he got off duty, he decided to have a little fun and placed a call to Malvina to reserve a girl for the evening. When he arrived, Malvina showed him three girls from which he could choose. They were all new recruits to her stable. Their young, tender vaginas didn't have a lot of mileage on them yet and were nice and tight, just the way Lucci liked his women. Out of the three girls, Lucci chose Gloria because she was more his type. She stood about six feet tall with a shapely set of long legs. She was bow legged with a nice gap between her thighs. Every woman he was ever with who had a gap like

Gloria had some good pussy so his selection was easy.

When he took her to one of the rooms at the brothel, he was even more impressed when she stripped down naked. Her body was even more amazing than he imagined. He instantly got hard just at the sight of her. When they got down to business, he wasn't inside of her for more than five minutes before the police burst into the room and had him and Gloria face down on the ground.

Lucci tried to tell the officers that he was a cop too in hopes they would give him a break, but they didn't care. This wasn't New York and he had no clout in New Jersey. He was handcuffed and thrown in the back of a paddy wagon just like everybody else in the brothel. His arrest made the news and he became a subject of shame and ridicule throughout NYPD. When he found out Gloria was underage, he knew he was screwed. Luckily, he had a good attorney and he managed to get three years probation instead of jail time. However, his career as a NYPD police officer was over.

Happy to have his freedom, Lucci decided to relocate to Baltimore to start a new life. Being a detective was the only legal skill set he had so he came up with the idea of starting a private investigation agency. One of his first clients happened to be Geno, whom he met through a mutual underworld associate. Geno hired him to dig up dirt on a dirty cop to help him win a police brutality case for one of his clients. Lucci delivered the goods for Geno and had been on retainer with him ever since. He was a lifesaver for Geno on numerous occasions and he was well paid for his services.

When Geno recently called him and asked him to find out information on a person named Jericho Jones, Lucci instantly went to work. He had an advantage over most private detectives because of his willingness to do whatever was necessary to get the information his client needed. He was street smart and had connections to underworld individuals most police detectives didn't. It didn't take him long to hit the jackpot and find out exactly what Geno requested.

When he reviewed the file he had on Jericho, he was sure Geno would be pleased with the results. He was waiting now for Geno to arrive to give him all of the background information he found on Jericho Jones. He had no idea what Geno wanted it for, but it didn't matter. Geno would surely reward him with a nice payday for his services rendered once he saw what he had for him. While he sipped on a cup of coffee, Geno arrived at his scheduled time. He hit the buzzer on his desk to let him into his office.

"Johnnie Boy, what do you know good? How's life been treating you?"

"Life is good, Geno. It will be even better once you see what I have for you."

"Well, let's get to it then."

Geno took a seat in the chair across from Lucci's desk inside of his compact sized office. Lucci's workplace was less than four hundred square feet, but it was just him and his secretary, Robin, who worked there. It was all the space they needed. Besides, Lucci spent most of his time out in the streets anyway. He handed Geno the file for him to review.

"I don't know why you wanted information on this guy, but let me tell you, he's bad news. I asked around on the streets and everybody says he's one cat you don't want to mess around with because he's a cold blooded killer. He calls himself The Smooth Assassin because when he kills his victims, he makes sure he leaves no trace of him ever being on the crime scene. He gets in and out in the blink of an eye. The police have never been able to pin a murder charge on him. He's like a ghost. I've had some friends of mine in New York who have used his services to do a hit. They say he's the real deal."

Geno looked over the information Lucci had in the folder while he listened to him talk. He was still trying to wrap his head around the fact that the man Lucci described was his half-brother. What was even more interesting was the more he described him, the more he sounded like he would fit right in as a member of the Caprese family. Their father was a contract killer and Jericho evidently inherited that skill set honestly. Even the way he killed his victims sounded similar to the way Leonardo used to describe some of the murders he committed. He wasn't the kind of hit man who left a trail of blood on a murder scene unless it was necessary. Leonardo told him he preferred to kill his victims fast and precise and make it appear like suicide or an accident as opposed to a murder. Jericho sounded like a chip off the old block. The more he read through the file, the more intrigued he became about Jericho. He still hated his father for betraying his mother, but he saw no reason to hold that against Jericho.

"Where can I find him?"

"Well, that's the thing; he's been missing in action for the past six months. Word on the street is his girlfriend is wanted for a murder and they split town. I hear he has a sister too and she left with them. Even though he is on the run, he still takes jobs occasionally. The only way to get a line to him is through a guy named Gutta. He's an old Vietnam Vet with a long rap sheet for all kinds of scandalous shit. He's a stone cold killer too, but not on the level of this Jericho cat. I have his information in the folder as well."

"Lucci, my man, you always deliver the goods. It's always a pleasure doing business with you."

Geno reached inside of his suit jacket and pulled out an envelope filled with cash. He didn't write him a check because this job was off the books. It had nothing to do with his law firm account. Lucci had no issue with being paid in cash. In fact, he preferred it that way.

"Likewise, Geno. Whenever you need the 411 on anybody, you know I'm your man."

Geno stood up and shook Lucci's hand. He made his exit with a renewed spirit about him. He had work to do. He planned to put his set up a meeting with Jericho through Gutta very soon. He imagined he would have as many questions for Geno as Geno had for him. He needed to see him face to face to gauge his temperature.

Chapter 24

Nesta sat at the bar of the Lemongrass Lounge, one of the many Caribbean restaurants that he owned, and awaited Geno's arrival. When he heard the voicemail message he left him, it sounded like vibrant reggae music to his ears. He had Geno positioned right where he wanted him to be. The big Boss man had to humble himself and come down off of his throne. Nesta had something he wanted badly. He planned to make Geno pay through the nose to get it if he wanted if bad enough. For all of the times he felt like he humiliated himself in an attempt to get Geno to give him a seat at his table, he would make Geno grovel and beg if he wanted him to hand over the knife which could possibly keep Cesare out of jail. As long Nesta had possession of it, he had Geno by the balls.

"Son, you make me so proud to call you my own flesh and blood."

"Thanks, Pops. I just want us to get our just due. At first Me respected Geno. I saw him as a stand up guy. I saw him as a shot caller and a true G. I liked the way him put him thing down and make the big business people respect his gangster, ya understand. But when he refused to show you the same respect you showed him, it ran me hot. Nobody can disrespect Me father and expect for Me not to have a problem with them. You taught me everything I know, Pops. Him treat your money like it don't spend the same as his. He act like this Jamaican shotta is not worthy of sitting next to him. Well, he will have to learn the hard way he will bow down to the King Nesta Clarke."

"I like the way you think there, son. Keep talking that talk."

Nesta felt proud to see Rah showed undying loyalty to him before anyone else. That was how he raised him to be. Rah never wavered from his respect for him or went against his wishes. He was a faithful son and field general. He would kill on the drop of a dime for his father. He placed no one before the bond they shared with one another. He would give his life before he betrayed Nesta.

"Sometimes things fall into your lap you never expected and become the biggest blessings in disguise. I remember when you told me when I was a little runt to never let an opportunity pass me by. If Me have to sell out some Yankee boy to help me father then so be it. Me not give a damn what nobody think."

When Rah came to Nesta with the bloody knife that had Cesare's fingerprints all over it, he didn't fully understand the power he put in his father's hands. Even though Cesare didn't kill Princess, the DNA evidence would make it appear like he did. His fingerprints on the knife would put him at the crime scene. This was a fact he denied vehemently to the police. He couldn't argue with the truth once the police ran his prints through their system and got a match.

It was bad enough for him the cops had it in bad for the Caprese family because Cesare was the least dangerous one of the bunch. He was only a threat to himself. He wouldn't harm a fly. However, if the police were to gain possession of the knife, his fate would be sealed. It wouldn't take much work for the State to make its case that Cesare killed Princess after they got into a violent confrontation given all of the prior altercations which were reported to the police. A guilty verdict would be easy to reach and Cesare would be assured a lengthy stint in state prison unless Geno chose to intervene and give Nesta something to make him happy in return for his brother's freedom.

The one thing both Rah and Nesta banked on was Geno loved Cesare enough to make a deal that would be to Nesta's liking. Even with Geno providing protection for him on the inside, both sides could agree Cesare wouldn't last in prison for long. He was too soft and lacked the street smarts to match wits with seasoned criminals who mastered the art of taking advantage of weak individuals like him. He was a prime candidate to become another man's bitch behind bars. They knew Geno was a proud man and he would do anything not to have his family's name disgraced in such a manner.

While he waited for Geno to arrive, Nesta thought about a potential problem he might have. If Geno were to offer him a piece of his deal to buy the L.A. Clippers, he would be in a position to take his organization to the next level as a corporate entity that could be one day comparable to the Caprese Foundation. If that happened, he would no longer have any need for the little arrangement he had agreed to with Silvio and Cappi. They no longer served a purpose for him. If he were to tell them the deal was off, he could expect some negative backlash to occur. He had just the right plan to insulate himself from having to deal with that issue. While he and Rah conversed, Geno and Sal walked into the lounge. They had several of their men with them for protection. They made their way over to the table where Nesta and Rah were seated.

"Ahhh, son, I see that our guests have arrived. Since it's your first time in my establishment, can I get you something to eat or drink? Our food is exquisite here. Just like you

Italians can make some mean dishes of food, we Jamaicans can do the same."

Nesta was cocky because he was in his territory where he was in a position of power and Geno had to respect his authority. It felt good to turn the tables on him, albeit it was just a temporary situation.

"Gentleman, we'll have to pass on the food. This is strictly a straight business meeting. There's no need for the extra stuff. I want to thank you for taking the time to meet with us today. There's no need to beat around the bush. You have something I need and I have something that you want. Let's see what we can negotiate."

"Geno, you are so used to calling the shots with everybody. However, you are now in my house. This is my establishment and I call the shots here. Have a seat and let me hear what you have to offer me to make this conversation worth my while."

Nesta loved controlling the exchange between him and Geno. He remained calm as he could in the face of this volatile situation. If it were not handled properly, things could go south very quickly and lead to a lot of people getting hurt badly. Neither side wanted the body count to rise among their respective crews because nobody won truthfully if they were to go to war. The most important thing to Geno was Cesare's freedom. As for Nesta, his focus was on business growth and prosperity. A happy medium had to be reached. Egos needed to be put aside to achieve progress amenable to both parties involved.

"Nesta, you tell me what you want and I will see if I can make it happen. You know what I want already. My brother's freedom is what's important to me."

"I want ten percent of that big deal you have going on to buy that NBA basketball team. I also want a seat at the table and to be able to buy a twenty percent interest in your foundation. With a seat on the board, I can be in on those big business deals you are always putting together. You let the Jackson brothers eat with you on the legal side of your business deals so why can't I eat as well? I'm just trying to level the playing field for myself. Can you make that happen?"

To own twenty percent of the foundation was unreasonable to Geno. To give away millions of dollars to someone who had not contributed one iota of assistance to helping him become successful was not going to happen. It would also make him lose his controlling interest in the business, which would diminish his power and influence to control the decision making. On top of that, he had to convince the entire board to approve the decision and he knew that would be a hard sell. Outside of Sal and the Jackson brothers, none of the other board members knew who Nesta was and wouldn't understand his recommendation to be a new board member.

"Ten percent is unreasonable. How about five percent of the Clippers deal if it goes through? I'll pay you out of my share of the team and it will be a deal just between me and you. I'll also kick you back a million dollars monthly out of the profits from the foundation, but I can't make you a partner. That's a lot of money Nesta. How does that sound?"

Nesta planned to rake him over the coals to no end. He realized Geno tried to lowball him. He had to show him he meant business. He could easily walk away from the table and just go through with the arrangement he made with Silvio and Cappi. It didn't matter to him. He would get what he wanted one way or another.

"It sounds like bullshit. I am not a fool. I won't let you brush me off like I'm some mid-level dope pusher. I'ma Boss just like you and I know you can do better than that offer. Because you disrespected me in my own establishment, I now want a twenty-five percent stake in the foundation and fifteen percent of the big deal. You can take the offer or leave it. If you don't agree to my terms, I can assure you this knife will land in the hands of the police by the morning and your brother will be going to jail for a long time. I will personally make sure he has a wicked stay for his entire bid. I'll give you a few minutes to talk it over with Sal."

Nesta and Rah walked away from the table so they could talk in private. Rah enjoyed the way his father took control of the entire meeting and set the terms. He got a good lesson on how to make a strong arm business maneuver behind the scenes just now.

"Geno, what are we going to do? I know you're not going to let him shake you down like that. I say we walk out of here and let Cesare do his time like a man and hold tight to what we have."

"Have you lost your mind? My brother is innocent. He will not be railroaded because of my bullshit. He's a fuckup, but he's blood. I've got this. Nesta thinks he's smart, but I'ma show him how smart he really is. He's not on my level. Take notes my friend. I'm about to give you a lesson on how to flex your muscle on a corporate level as opposed to in the streets. I didn't get myself in this position by accident. Watch and learn, Sal."

Geno was livid and ripe to exact revenge upon Nesta for what he was trying to do to him. He essentially wanted to usurp his authority and render him a non-factor in his own foundation. He wanted to humiliate him in front of his own team to be shook down in such a manner. He couldn't go out like that. He had to stand his ground. If he gave into Nesta's demands he would be ruined. He had to play hardball with him and call his bluff. He figured Nesta was grandstanding and attempting to gauge how much Geno was willing to sacrifice to save his brother's life. He was about to find out how shrewd Geno was. He motioned for Nesta and Rah to come back over to the table.

"Look Nesta let's be real about this. You know damn well you are not getting twenty-five percent of my company under any condition. You would have to kill me first to make that happen. Let's be reasonable here. I can admit you have me in a compromising situation and have me in a position where I know I have to give something up to get what I want. I'm willing to give you seven percent and that's my final offer. I will still pay you the million dollars every month in exchange for what I want. You can take it or leave it. I love my brother dearly the same way you love your son, but I will not let you bend me over and rape me like a little school girl. I'm Geno Caprese. My offer is my final one. If you don't take it, then we will go to war. I will spare no expense to crush your entire team. I won't rest until everyone you love is dead and in the dirt. You know I'm not bluffing. I have the reach and the resources to do exactly what I said I planned to do. I can either make you a richer man and we both walk away from this table happy or I can make you a dead man. The choice is yours."

Everybody at the table had a stunned look on their faces. Out of nowhere, Geno shifted the entire tide of the conversation. Sal had no clue where Geno was going with his hard ball stance, but he would ride or die with him regardless. Rah observed in disbelief that Geno could be so bold in the face of the fire. He waited eagerly to see his father's next move. Nesta thought for second before he spoke.

"You have yourself a deal, Geno."

"I'll have the paperwork drawn up today. I'll expect you will be sending a package my way as well. I'm glad we could come to an agreement. I would like to think we are both sensible men. Now that the deal is done, we'll be on our way," Geno stated authoritatively. He shook hands with Nesta to solidify the deal. His next move was to get to work on Cesare's case.

"Geno, before you leave, I have one more thing for you. This is a gift from me to you. You may want to clean out your house because there are a few snakes in there you need to keep your eyes on. Your brother and Cappi tried to cut a side deal with me to get rid of you."

Geno was caught off guard by Nesta's confession. After he thought about it for a moment, he wasn't surprised at all. Silvio had never let go of his desire to sit in Geno's seat. He was, however, surprised Cappi would follow suit to be in cahoots with him. Nonetheless, Geno would respond accordingly to the information Nesta just dropped on him.

"I appreciate the heads up. You gentleman have a good day."

Geno and Sal exited the lounge. He was headed back to the office to draw up the paperwork for Nesta and to handle a few other things.

"Pops, what the hell did you just do? You had all of the cards and you let him walk away giving you just chump change?"

"You see this is why I'm the teacher and you're still the student. I didn't let him walk away at all. I knew he would never give me what I asked for from the start. However, when you negotiate with men like Geno you have to make them think they are always in control when they agree to the terms you wanted initially. He exceeded my expectations by far. With his offer, we will make tens of millions of dollars and we have to do absolutely nothing but sit back and collect the money. Now, son, you tell me, who's the fool?"

Rah thought about the jewel his father just dropped on him. It now made sense. He just got a lesson in back room dealing which would serve him well in the future.

"That was pure genius, Pops. However, why did you give him the info on his brother and Cappi?"

"I gave them up because they are of no use to me any longer. I got what I wanted. Once they find out the arrangement we made is now null and void, they'll be out for revenge. That could've been another problem I would have to address. Now that Geno knows about them, he will deal with them accordingly. They are now his headache."

"I get it now. You killed two birds with one stone. I didn't think of it that way. Well, cheers to Geno Caprese for making us even richer than we already are!" Rah exclaimed excitedly. He ordered drinks from the bar for them to celebrate. Little did he know his celebration was premature. Things never went according to plans in back door deals. There were always unforeseen bumps in the road that came along.

Chapter 25

Geno was successful in getting the murder charge against Cesare dropped. The State had a very flimsy case against him from the very beginning. The only reason they came after him in the first place was because of his family ties. The police department was determined to railroad Cesare with a trumped up charge just to say they were able to get a conviction against one member of the Caprese family. If he didn't have a brother who was the fiercest attorney in the City and who was also wealthy with a lot of clout, there plan might have worked.

The penal system across America is filled with a countless number of individuals that were innocent of the charges brought against them, but they lacked the financial resources to hire a top notch attorney to defend them. They were routinely stuck with a public defender that saw them as just another case number in their huge caseloads. The State paid their salaries and they had no motivation to go the extra mile to put forth a viable defense for these individuals. As a result, they routinely wound up being unjustly convicted of a crime they didn't commit and were sentenced to lengthy prison sentences as a punishment.

The police had no DNA evidence or a witness that could put Cesare at the scene of the crime during the timeframe in which Princess died. They also didn't have the knife that killed Princess. It was handed over to Geno once the ink dried on the contract he sent to Nesta to solidify their new business arrangement. Geno made sure the police would never get a chance to find the knife because he destroyed it himself. It was no longer an issue in this case.

The crime scene expert that Geno had on retainer gave him a certified statement which indicated that the knife wound in Princess's chest appeared to be self-inflicted judging by the angle of entry. He also stated that the person who did the stabbing was right handed. That eliminated Cesare because he was left handed. The medical examiner, Dr. Ramona Dixon, reached the same conclusion, but the district attorney attempted to have her change her statement. Dr. Dixon refused to do so because she was a woman of integrity and upstanding character.

When one of Geno's spies inside of the D.A.'s office tipped him off to the attempted cover up, he threatened to sue the State for its actions.

In response to his threat, the case was quickly dropped to save all of the guilty parties involved from the embarrassment he would cause them when he went on a media blitz about the unjust nature of the charges leveled against Cesare.

As for Princess, her family would never know what truly happened to her. They held on to the belief it was Cesare who killed her, but he got away with murder thanks to Geno. Her mother swore to dedicate the rest of her life to getting justice for her daughter. She was too blinded by her emotions at the moment to see her energy was being wasted on a lost cause. Her daughter's death was a tragic accident, but in no way was it murder. It was a bitter pill to swallow, but it was the truth.

Happy to be free, Cesare stood outside in front of the jail and waited for Geno to come pick him up. The time he spent behind bars gave Cesare plenty of time to think about his life. He had been to jail numerous times in the past for petty charges, but to face a murder charge was an eye opening experience for him. It made him realize just how quickly a bad decision could alter the entire course of one's life.

The thought of him spending a huge chunk of his life behind bars made him realize how short life was and how much time he had already wasted doing absolutely nothing productive. He was surrounded by individuals in jail who had already served years behind bars and had nothing to lose. He witnessed inmates getting raped and brutally beaten on a daily basis. He, of course, was safe for now in the city jail because of his family's reputation. Everybody feared Geno's wrath if they laid a hand on Cesare. However, if he were convicted and sent to state prison, he would just be another DOC number amongst thousands of others. He would face the same deadly risks as any other inmate in the system. This experience was a wakeup call he desperately needed.

The way Geno went to bat for him throughout this ordeal, from being his attorney to making a deal with the devil, in the form of Nesta, to save his life, he honestly had to re-evaluate his perception of him. He no longer saw him as being hard on him, but realized he had his best interest at heart at all times. He just wanted him to get his life together so he could live a purpose driven existence. He wanted him to become more responsible in the choices he made. Geno didn't want to just give him everything in life, but he wanted him to earn his keep like most men did, whether it was in a legal or illegal manner.

Even with his new outlook on life, there was one piece of unfinished business he wanted to handle. He wanted to pay Rah back for turning his back on him. He was supposed to be his best friend. Geno advised him to leave the situation alone because he would handle it, but Cesare couldn't let it go. The feeling of betrayal ran deep for Cesare. He wanted revenge and had it in the back of his mind to give Rah his just due at the proper time.

As for Silvio, he never came to see him or answered any of his calls while he was locked up. He started to feel like Geno was right when he told him how self-centered Silvio was. He didn't want to believe it was true, but he saw no other explanation as to why the brother he thought he was the closest to wasn't around in the most trying time in his young life. The more he thought about it, the angrier he became. He took one last hail off of the cigarette he had in his hand before he tossed it to the ground. Geno had just arrived to pick him up in his Corvette. He was happy to see him.

"Come here, man. I'm glad you're home. Didn't I tell you I would come through for you?" Geno asked.

Geno got out of his car and ran over to the curb to give him a hug. He was glad that Cesare was finally free because he didn't deserve to be in jail in the first place. He noticed he had put on a little weight. He wasn't fat, but a little pudgy around the midsection. It didn't matter. As long as he wasn't still stuck up in a jail cell, Geno was content.

"Yeah you did tell me to have faith in you. I'm grateful for everything you did for me, Geno."

"I hope you learned a lesson from this, C."

"I sure did. Do me a favor Geno and don't call me C anymore. You can call me Cesare from now on. I have a new attitude about life now. I'm ready to deal with the world like a grown up and not a reckless teenager anymore."

"That's what I'm talking about, lil' bro. That's all I've wanted to hear from you all of this time. Whatever you want to do, you know I've got your back."

"Being locked up in a cell made me appreciate my life and see I've got to do things different if I want something different. I think I'm going to enroll in college next semester and take a few classes. What do you think?"

Geno almost crashed his car when he heard the word "college" come out of Cesare's mouth. He wondered if his brother had been abducted by an alien or something because the man before him didn't sound like the Cesare he knew.

"I think that's a damn good idea. However, what about your music?"

"I'm done with that pipe dream. I always knew I sucked as a rapper, but I didn't want to admit it to myself. I just wanted to become a rap superstar and have people see me as being someone special. I wanted people to respect me the way they respect you and Sil."

"Let me tell you something lil' bro and I want you to hear me clearly. Fuck what anybody else thinks about you. As long as you know what you want and are willing to put in the work to get it, they don't matter. That holds true in the streets and in the business world. Do you think I got to be where I am worrying about what other people think? Shit, when we were growing up, Silvio used to always test me because he thought I was soft. Once I stood my ground and held my own in a fight with him, he had to respect me. Cesare, what I'm saying is this: if you want respect from people, don't ask for it, just be you and do your best and the respect will come your way."

"That makes perfect sense. I know I didn't use to listen to you, but trust me, I'm listening now."

Geno beamed with pride at the sight of his little brother. If he was serious about going to school, he would help him in any way he could. This was the realest and deepest conversation they ever had as they rode back to Geno's house. Cesare would be staying with him for a while until he was back up on his feet. Being around Carina and his family would do him some good.

Chapter 26

Lila's was packed to capacity tonight. All of the city's young hustlers were in the building. They competed with each other to see who could spend the most money by making it rain for the sexy exotic dancers. Cappi was a happy man at the moment because when the club was packed like it was tonight, the customers brought round after round of drinks. The crowd was so big because it was a birthday celebration for Moreno, one of the top lieutenants in the Jackson crew. All of his boys came out to show him love and to have a good time smacking on some fat asses and balling out like true playboys were supposed to do.

Although he was a well respected drug dealer, Moreno originally made a name for himself as an R&B singer. He had a few hit records when he was signed to a small, independent local record label. His music created such a buzz regionally that he and his manager, Stokey, were in negotiations with Warner Brothers to sign a distribution deal until he experienced a life changing tragedy. He got caught in the bed with another man's woman and the dude slit his throat with a razor. His vocal cords were damaged in the process, thus ruining his chance at superstardom. He was crushed when the doctors told him the news. With music no longer an avenue to success for him, he dove full throttle into the drug game with his cousins, Milton and Jarvis Jackson. Over time, he became one of their most trusted soldiers.

While the music blasted through the speakers, everybody had a good time. It was all love throughout the place. Around midnight, Silvio strolled into the club. He usually showed up around that time and stayed until closing to be able to take Sparkle home with him. Since they first met, they grew to be close and were now an item. Silvio wasn't normally the kind of gangster to fall in love, but Sparkle had a way about her that got his nose open. It was so bad at one point that when he would see her up on stage dancing for customers and they got a little too friendly for his taste, he found himself in a jealous rage. He got into several fights with random dudes over her.

Silvio's jealousy got so bad Cappi had to intervene and remind him that her flirting with customers was strictly business and nothing personal. Over time, his message sunk in with him. Tonight when he walked in the club and saw her up on the stage being friendly with a customer, he just turned and walked away toward Cappi's office in the back of the lounge. Cappi was already in his office watching everything that went down on the security monitors in front of him.

"The place is jumping tonight, Cappi! How much do you think you'll take down by closing?"

"I would say at least five grand off of the door and another seven to ten grand in drinks. That's not bad for one night. I wish every night was like this."

"I hear you, man. I did pretty well this week myself. I got rid of a truck load of electronic equipment the other day."

"That's good right there. I have to be honest with you, Sil; this place has run real smoothly without your brother around. Now that he's home, I hope Geno doesn't send him back here."

"You don't have to worry about that, Cappi. I called him the other day when I found out he was home. I found out he was mad with me because I didn't come see him while he was locked up for that little stretch. I told him I was busy and he needed to man up. Shit, I can't hold his hand and walk him through every situation in life. Needless to say, I don't think you'll have to worry about him coming around here anytime soon. He's so far up Geno's ass right now this place is not even on his radar."

"Well, that's good news. So, when are we going to set this plan in motion?"

"I'm waiting to hear back from Nesta. I called him a few times this week, but he hasn't returned my calls."

"That's not a good look. We need to get a move on if we are going to make it happen. Holy shit....speak of the devil. Look who just walked in the club."

When Cappi looked up on the monitor, he was surprised to see Geno walk into the lounge along with Milton and Jarvis. Geno never came down to the strip club because he viewed it as a second rate business establishment. However, he had no problem accepting his monthly kickback from Cappi. Second rate or not, the money spent the same way for him. The three men were headed directly for Cappi's office. He had no clue what they wanted. When they entered Cappi's office, they all wore serious looks on their faces. Geno turned toward Silvio and attempted to hug him. Silvio was hesitant but hugged him back.

"So, what's up, Sil? How have you been my big brother? How are things going for you, Cappi? Are you guys alright down here? It seems like all of the action is upstairs."

"Yeah, I'm good bro. It's packed upstairs. We decided to come down here to relax. Besides, I wouldn't want to steal all of the girls' attention from the guest of honor," Silvio joked while he glanced in Milton and Jarvis' direction.

"I don't think you have to worry about that, Sil. Moreno can hold his own with the ladies. Trust me, you are no threat to him," Jarvis stated directly. It was clear there was tension in the air. Cappi tried to break the ice.

"So, what brings you down here, Geno?" Cappi asked getting right to the point. He knew something had to be up for Geno to show his face in one of his least favorite places.

"Well, I just had a burning desire to see you two in person. I wanted to look you both in the eyes to let you know you have been expelled from the family."

"Expelled? What the hell are you talking about, Geno?" Silvio interjected with a slight hint of laughter in his voice.

"You heard me correctly. You see, a little birdie put a bug in my ear and said you two geniuses have been trying to cut a side deal with the enemy to take over my position in this family. Yes, I'm talking about Nesta. I know all about your little plan."

Silvio and Cappi both instantly tensed up. They were scared as hell. They had been exposed. Silvio now knew why he hadn't heard from Nesta. He had ratted them out and hung them out to dry.

"I don't know what you heard, bro, but...." Silvio tried to explain before Geno cut him off in mid-sentence.

"Save me the bullshit, Sil. I know you. You're the same thirsty, muscle headed bastard you've always been all of your life. You have always wanted your spot back as the head of this family since I took it from you while you were locked up. The cold hard reality is you are just not smart enough to run this crew like I can and you can't accept that truth," Geno insulted him.

When Silvio heard those words, he became enraged. He lunged toward Geno to throw a punch, but Geno moved out of the way before he connected. Jarvis and Milton jumped into the fight and pinned Silvio down on the floor.

"Get the fuck off of me, nigga. Get your monkey hands off of me!" Silvio yelled at Milton and Jarvis.

"Ahhh, keep talking. Tell us how you really feel," Jarvis egged Silvio on with his knee in his back. Silvio was helpless.

"Cappi, I'm surprised he convinced you to go along with his scheme. We used to be close at one time."

"Yeah, we were close, Geno, but then you went all Hollywood on us. You lost your soul and turned your back on the streets and forgot where you came from ever since you became a lawyer."

"That is stupidest thing I have ever heard. I'm not even entertaining this bullshit. This is how it's going to go. I'm giving you both an hour to pack all of your shit and get the fuck out of town for good. Milton will be taking over Lila's from here on out from you Cappi. You're fired. The only reason I don't kill you both is because I'm in a good mood. Now, if you don't do as I say, do you see all of those young Black men out there having a good time spending a lot of money? I sent them all here tonight. I arranged this party. It's your going away party. If you don't do as I say, I'ma let them have at you two and it won't be pretty. Silvio, I dare you to use the word nigga in front of that group of young lions. Watch how fast they tear you a new asshole. Fellas, so what's it gonna be?"

"I'm going. You'll never hear from me again in life. That's a promise," Cappi stated out of pure fear. He was smart enough to recognize Geno could easily kill him for his betrayal, but he gave him a pass. He planned to take it and gracefully move on. He got up from behind his desk and made a beeline for the door to exit before Geno changed his mind.

"You're gonna regret this move, Geno. I promise you that," Silvio stated resolutely.

"You know, Sil, you still don't see the big picture. You never have and, unfortunately, never will. I can see that if I let you go, you'll find a way to become a pain in my ass. Fellas, you can do what you want with this one. I don't care. Silvio, tell Satan I said hello," Geno stated coldly.

Those were the last words he spoke to Silvio. Milton and Jarvis planned to make his death a drawn out and painful process. They had Rome and Dre waiting outside in a van to take Silvio to a place they called The Redrum room. It was located in an abandoned warehouse they owned in a remote section of South Baltimore. Redrum was the word murder spelled backwards. Countless murders and torturing of informants took place there. Geno felt no guilt ordering the murder of his own brother because he earned his fate honestly by being a lying backstabber. Silvio was one more enemy he crossed off his list with a few more to go.

Chapter 27

Since he sent the contract back to Geno to solidify their agreement, Nesta felt like he was on top of the world. He would soon be wealthy beyond his wildest dreams if Geno pulled off this big deal. Until then, the one million dollar monthly payment he would receive would suffice. He was proud of the way he maneuvered Geno right into position where he wanted him to extort him in a manner Geno was famous for doing to others.

Nesta believed he played Geno like the pawn on the chessboard and did so masterfully. A man who was perceived as invincible and untouchable by so many was made to humble himself by a skinny Black boy from the island of Jamaica. Nesta was overflowing with a new level of confidence in his position as a major player in both the streets and the business world. By taking on Geno, he was battle tested because, in his view, he came through the storm without a dent in his armor.

To celebrate his success, Nesta had a big cookout at his large mansion located in the West Baltimore County community known as Lochearn. He invited all of his workers and business partners to come join in on his celebration. His personal chef manned the grill and cooked a feast that consisted of all of his favorite Caribbean dishes. Nesta only knew how to do things big and in grand fashion. He hired a live reggae band to play music all night long. He flew in a fleet of beautiful women straight from the island of Jamaica. Their only purpose was to provide pleasure and companionship for his soldiers. As hard as he pushed his workers to earn out in the streets, they deserved a day to unwind by eating some good food and getting some good home grown poom poom.

Liddell even showed up for the party. He acted as though everything was copacetic between them even though that was far from the truth. He still had plans to kill Nesta, but he had to wait until the time was right. Plus, when Nesta told him about his new arrangement with Geno and how Silvio and Cappi approached him about bringing Geno a move, he was glad he did wait. He was upset Nesta didn't cut him in on the deal he negotiated, but he played it off as though it didn't matter. Nesta's selfish actions only reinforced to Liddell why he had to look out for himself. Since he hadn't heard from Silvio or Cappi and Nesta told him he gave them up to Geno, he just assumed that they were dead or would be soon. It made no difference to him because he didn't need them to do what he had in mind. They were replaceable parts in a much grander scheme.

"Is everybody having a good time?" Nesta asked over the microphone. He was on his fifth Rum punch and as drunk as could be. He didn't care because he was safe at home among his own people. At least, that's what he thought. The crowd responded with a unanimous "Yes" to his question. The men were dressed in their swimming trunks and the ladies were scantily clad in g-string bikinis. They didn't need to go to Hedonism in Jamaica to experience uninhibited sexual fun. Nesta brought Hedonism to them at his large estate, which had more than enough room in the house and on the surrounding perimeter for everyone to indulge their sexual fantasies.

Not to be left out of the fun, Nesta busied himself with two thick legged women on a lounge chair by the pool. He had both of his hands wrapped around the butt of one woman while the other one filled his mouth with her breasts. His penis was rock hard and ready for action. However, he didn't want to rush a good thing so he enjoyed the foreplay for the moment. They had the rest of the night to do whatever came to mind.

While the party was in full swing, a delivery man arrived with a package for Nesta. One of his soldiers signed for it and brought it to Nesta. When he looked at the package, he was confused as to where it came from because it didn't have a return address on it. He ripped the paper off of the package and opened the box. Inside of the box, there was a box of Montecristo cigars, the kind he remembered Geno smoked.

Nesta sobered up quickly, but it was too late. Before he could react, the box exploded in his hands. His entire estate was blown into tiny pieces by the bomb. Nesta, along with all of his guests, were killed. The only one who wasn't dead out of his crew was Rah and that was because he wasn't at the party due to being on a journalism assignment in Trinidad. With such a massive body count at one time, Geno wanted to send a clear message to the streets- he was the Boss of all bosses without question. After this act, it couldn't have been made more official.

Chapter 28

Now that the drama in his daily life had died down, Geno felt free to enjoy his life a little bit. For the last few weeks since he rid himself of his enemies, he decided to take a break from work to relax. He spent his evenings at home with his children watching movies and even found time for him and Carina to go out on several dates like they used to do when they first met. He was content with appreciating the simple things life. However, he knew his current state of tranquility wouldn't last forever because of who he was. As much as he wanted to be a normal guy at times, in the real world, he was a powerful man, at the head of a successful business empire with a gang of employees that depended upon him. He also had a gang of street soldiers who hung on his every word. He was too much of a true leader to let them down.

Geno was a bit irritated that his bid to buy the Los Angeles Clippers was at a stalemate. As it turns out, the loony owner of the team, Donald Sterling, planned to legally challenge his lifetime ban by the NBA and to contest their efforts to make him sell the team by filing a lawsuit. Even though he was upset because he worked hard at gathering the right people to the table to try and make a go at this deal, he didn't let it distract him from his overall goal, which was to increase the financial holdings of the Caprese Foundation. He had several other irons in the fire, though not as promising as the possible purchase of an NBA team, which could prove to be lucrative ventures.

Geno was happy he and Cesare got a chance to connect like brothers should. They talked more recently than they did in all of their earlier years. Cesare joined him when he had his kickboxing training sessions with Rico in his basement gym. It was hard for him to keep up with Rico and Geno because he was out of shape and a mere novice. However, Geno was happy just to have him there. At least he knew where he was and that he was safe.

Geno decided to tell Cesare about his conversation he had with their father about his two illegitimate children. Cesare was just as stunned as Geno was when Leonardo told him the news. Geno talked with his mother recently. She tried to get him to talk to his father, but he had no desire whatsoever to do so. Their relationship was irreparably damaged.

Geno didn't give Cesare all of the details he got from Lucci about Jericho because he didn't deem it to be necessary at this time. Cesare was as anxious to meet Jericho and Shavon. They were all around the same age and he was sure they had a lot in common. Geno had yet to hear back from his people about a meeting being set up between him and Jericho so he continued to patiently wait until it was arranged.

Geno put all of his big business plans to the side tonight. It was family time. Tonight was all about Gianna. He and Carina were in attendance at a big fashion event sponsored by local designer Marco Rinaldi. Gianna was one of the featured models he selected to model some of his latest designs. This was her first major modeling assignment and she was beyond excited.

When the show started and Geno saw Gianna walk down the runway like a seasoned model, he was proud of her. That was his baby girl up on the stage and she held her own with all of the other models that were far more seasoned and experienced than her. When the show was over, they all planned to go out to have dinner to celebrate. As they were about to leave, Geno had a pressing urge to go to the bathroom. He excused himself and made his way to the men's room.

When he made it to the urinal, Geno felt like

a ton of bricks were lifted off of his back after he urinated. He had to go to the bathroom since the beginning of the show, but held it in because he didn't want to miss Gianna when she came on the stage. As he was about to walk toward the sink to wash his hands, he noticed a tall, Black male a few stalls down staring in his direction. They were the only two people in the bathroom. The man followed closely behind him and used the sink next to Geno.

"How are you today, sir?" the man said to Geno. Geno normally didn't speak to strangers, but the guy seemed harmless.

"I'm fine and yourself?" he asked in return while he dried his hands.

"I'm doing well. I understand you've been looking for me?" the man inquired.

Geno was thrown off guard because the tone of the man's voice changed from harmless to creepy just that quickly. He felt some comfort that he had his gun on him just in case the man wanted some drama.

"Do I know you, buddy?" he asked while he tried to place his face.

"No, you don't know me, but I've been studying you and your family my whole life. My name is Jericho Jones. It's nice to meet you, Geno," Jericho said as he revealed himself.

Geno felt nervous and tried to reach for his gun, but he was too slow. Jericho already had the drop on him. He had his gun in his hand ready to squeeze the trigger. He had a sinister look in his eyes. Geno braced himself because he knew that his death was near.......

To be continued

Comments/Notes

Other titles available by Thomas Long:

Dayvon's Story: A Thug's Life
Just Like Daddy
Money Kings: Just Like Daddy 2
Takeisha's Song: Cash Rules Everything
Unconventional Love
The Bodymore Homicide Novella series
Love TKO
High Society Gangster II: The Caprese Family

You can also find out additional information on
Thomas Long at:

www.tlongwrites.com

http://www.tlongwrites.com/apps/blog

http://www.amazon.com/Thomas-
Long/e/B0058OVYC6/

Facebook:

https://www.facebook.com/pages/Thomas-
Long/169575816453538

Twitter and Instagram: @tlongmoney

Available September 2015!

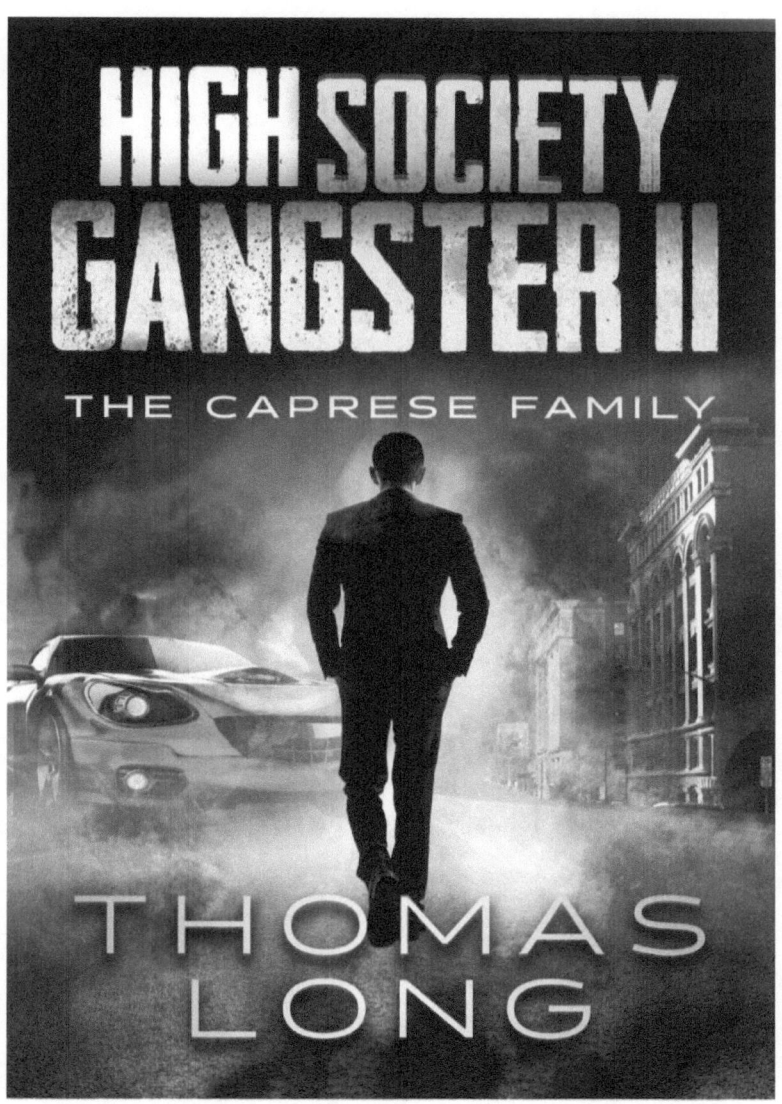